Eternally Star-Crossed Haters

Casey Nash

Published by Casey Nash, 2022.

ETERNALLY STAR-CROSSED HATERS

First edition. July 1, 2022.

ISBN: 979-8201701482

Written by Casey Nash.

Table of Contents

This book is dedicated to my kindergarten teacher Denise Webb who told me she would come to my book signing when I published a book, my childhood librarians Jane Devereaux and Ms. Coe, and to my mom and dad. All of these adults told me stories that helped teach me to become a story teller.

Prologue

The teens sat across from each other at a nondescript, beige table. The walls were a white mist, an ornate oval mirror was hovering on one side to make the space seem larger. In the far corner was an exotic potted plant with blue hued leaves. The room had no doors. Both were nude. They sat with their legs crossed and the girl had her arms folded and eyes closed. The boy stared at the backs of his hands laying flat on the table.

Their counselor had a stack of folders on the table more than a foot high, with numerous post it notes defeating their purpose of organization. Behind him was a large fish tank with silvery green fish and a small sign identifying them as "*Sarotherodon galilaeus*". He was wearing a simple grey cassock. Everything was silent while the teens sat and the counselor wrote scrupulous notes.

When he was finished, he put a cap on his pen, filed the paper away and looked at the two teens.

"Thirty lives. Over four hundred years. Uncountable murders, tragedies, and legends. All over one curse. What do you have to say for yourselves?" the man asked both of them. He had rounded, tortoise shell, horn rimmed glasses which he took off and placed on top of the papers.

The girl opened her eyes, blinked, and glowered. The boy sighed and sat up in his seat a bit taller.

"For starters, her family is always completely unreasonable. They are so controlling and untrusting. They keep her under a rock and won't let her form an opinion which causes her to be a completely vapid airhead." The young man avoided looking at the girl while he spoke.

"Oh, sure, blame me. But, honestly? If you weren't such an immature, impulsive, horndog we would never get into the problems that happen. And my families are unreasonable? My families have always done what is proper and correct, while your family is self centered and greedy." The girl kicked the table leg as she finished talking.

"Please. Enough. Calm down," the man said standing, "There has been enough fighting for all life times. You still need to work together to break this curse and get out of purgatory. You live for almost twenty years, almost get your happy ending, and then wind right back up here waiting to be reincarnated again."

The man paced while straightening his beard and the gold and silver keys on a cord around his neck. He picked up his staff to carry as he walked across the room.

"What are we going to do then, Pete?" The boy asked with a haughty air. The girl rolled her eyes.

"Oh there is no we. I'm not cursed, though it might feel like it. This is all up to the both of you." he gestured at both of the teens. "I have the power to make little changes here and there, but I can't control free will or force people to love each other."

"Well, it would help if our families didn't hate each other. That always makes it a struggle. Give them something in common," the girl stared right at the counselor while she spoke, ignoring the boy, "And try to give Romeo a bit of common sense and rationality! He should be more serious and have some kind of grand life ambition."

The boy scoffed and laughed, "She shouldn't be so innocent and straight laced. I have no idea how our families could get along, they haven't in almost half a millennia no matter what kind of humans we have been. I am tired of dying. I want to live a complete life, and then just retire from this. With or without her."

"Without you would be my paradise!"

"Mine, too, I can't believe how many times I've died for you!"

"Enough!" the man tapped the table with his staff, "Romeo, you will be reincarnated first. Juliet, you will come second. We tried to have you be older last time with no better results. Your families this time will have no feud. In fact, they are old friends. Your mothers grew up very close, traveled apart, but are now back in the same small town. Are you ready? Anything else before we try again?"

"Ready when you are," Romeo said with a sardonic smile. Juliet mimicked him with a screwed up face as the counselor pointed at him with his staff and he faded into mist.

"Right. We'll give it some time to let him age up. Good luck, I really, really am rooting for the both of you." The counselor flipped the many tabbed folders while he spoke.

"We need as much help as we can get," Juliet said as she, too, dissipated out of one realm and back into the mortal one.

1 Romeo

"Roman! Honey! You only have a few more minutes until we have to leave."

Roman's mom paced outside his bedroom door while she straightened her polka dotted dress. She knew that her and her son needed to get to the school early so he could register for his senior year classes. The door opened abruptly.

"It's fine, really Mom, I already have all the credits planned out. Conditioning, AP courses, a few concurrent college credit classes. A full schedule that will be great on my college admissions."

"Honey, I wish you wouldn't push yourself so hard. This is going to be your last year of high school. You should have fun and enjoy yourself, there is your entire life ahead of you to fill up with work."

"Mom, if I don't set myself up for my future now I won't be able to retire with multiple investment funds. I have a plan with contingencies and back ups. A lot of work now for fun and relaxation later."

It was the same discussion they had had time and time again. Roman's mother turned down the hallway and grabbed her purse and keys. They walked to their grey minivan and drove through the neighborhood. Roman had been looking through different college come-on pamphlets and looked up as they came to a traffic light.

"Mom, this isn't the way to the school. What are you doing?"

"Oh I thought I told you. Julianna is going to your school this year. Her mom is still at work today and so she is going to stay with me until freshman orientation and registration starts this afternoon."

"What? Oh man, Mom, you know she is so weird. I thought they were still living out of state."

"Her dad got transferred to a new base overseas and so they are back home. They just got back a few weeks ago. Charles only has a few months of service left before being discharged so Angelica is coming home ahead of time, partially so Julianna can start the year off and not have to change halfway through."

Roman groaned and buried his nose back into the stacks of papers. Julianna had always been annoying and clingy when they had been forced to socialize as little kids. He hadn't seen her since he was in junior high. He hoped she still wouldn't prattle on incessantly.

The van rolled up into the driveway and a girl stood up from the front stoop and shrugged a satchel bag onto her shoulder. Her hair was short and spiky on the left side and pitch black. On the right side it hung to her waist with purple streaks through it. There were multiple piercings in her left ear. She wore baggy, black pants and a band shirt that had "Mooseknuckle Sandwich" written across it. Roman was sitting in complete shock, if he hadn't been to their house as a kid he would have thought they had made a mistake. His mom leaned over and gently smacked him in the arm.

"Where are your manners? Get out and open the door for her. Now!"

Roman got out and held onto his own papers and bag. He wordlessly held the door for her while just staring.

Julianna looked him over and said, "Thanks. Hi Mrs. Montero, thanks for the ride. I really appreciate it," as she climbed into the car. The last time they had seen each other Julianna had been about eight years old. Roman had been short for a sixth grader and they had been about eye to eye. She often had teased him about being older, but shorter than her, when he still was an inch or two taller than her. His height had more than made up for what it had been lacking. He was just over six foot two and was uncomfortable when riding in the back seat. It felt like his knees were going into his ears. The Carpenters had been gone ever since the year Roman had started junior high. He hadn't really missed them, and still got unsolicited updates from his mom every few days.

Roman made sure Julianna was completely settled in the front seat as he closed the door and saw that she also had a guitar case with her. It almost hadn't crossed his mind that she was supposedly some sort of prodigy virtuoso. The last time her mom had his family over to listen to her play she was still learning the piano. He silently prayed that his family wouldn't be invited over to listen to any more of Julianna's little concerts. In the middle portion of the van he got his seat belt on and started reading the next pamphlet.

"It's so nice to see you Julianna! I can't wait to spend more time with you and your mom. We really have a lot to catch up on." Roman's mom smiled over at Julianna as they backed out of the carport. From the back seat Roman closed his eyes and cursed his luck. His mom was going to force small talk the entire way to the school.

"Yeah, Mrs. Montero, mom is super psyched to be back in town. I'm sure we'll be over as much as her work schedule allows. She really wants to make a good impression with her bosses at the gallery."

"Oh dear, you know you can call me Val. I know it's been a long time since we've seen each other, but I think of you just like a daughter. It is so wonderful you and Romey will be at the same school together. I'm sure if you need anything you can find him and he will be happy to help you with anything you need. Right, Romey?"

Roman grunted, there was a slightly threatening tone to his mother's inflection, "Yes, Mom. And don't call me Romey."

Every time she called him Romey around other kids it would get stuck for weeks of teasing. It sounded like he was a roaming cell phone. Rome EEEE! He was hoping that if nobody brought it up again this year and through college it would die completely. Thank god. The more he protested it the more it stuck, but it was grating to have it pushed on him again and again.

"I don't know if your mother told you, Julianna, but Romey here is going to be offered full ride scholarships to different universities after this year. He is the absolute star of the boy's volleyball and basketball teams! Games will be starting soon and we can go with your mom. Are you going to try out for any sports, maybe cheerleading?"

Roman and Julianna both stifled laughs. It was a good thing Roman was in the back seat and hidden behind his stack of papers. His mom was out of her mind thinking a girl like that would ever want to be, much less make, the cheerleading team. He hated the way she talked about him like he wasn't even there and every accomplishment he made was instantly something for her to make herself seem more interesting and important.

"Actually, I think I'll be pretty busy with drama and guitar. I heard the school also has some steel band class, but I think joining guitar class would be better. I brought my acoustic in case they need a demonstration for me to place into a higher level than beginner."

"That's fantastic you are taking such fun classes! I wish Romey would stop taking himself so seriously and just enjoy being a kid while he can."

"I enjoy myself fine, Mom, drama and music are not my thing. I would be completely out of my comfort zone."

"Drama and guitar aren't just some "for fun" classes, Val. I plan on doing a lot after high school and taking courses that can build my public speaking skills will be really helpful. I take my art pretty seriously."

Roman knew he was only a few years older than Julianna, but hearing this thirteen year old, about-to-be freshman talking about taking her music and drama courses seriously made him feel very mature. Taking a bunch of fine arts courses was well and good, but serious? Serious plans included something that would affect the world at a broad level, not playing some music and acting in some play.

"Of course Julianna, I didn't mean that they aren't important, but Roman has taken just about every science and math course the school offers. I tried to tell him to take it easy this year with more electives or taking a smaller course load, but he doubled up on concurrent courses at the community college and AP classes."

"Mom, the more credits I get now, the faster I can get started on my masters and doctorates. The sooner I graduate and enter the workforce the better, I don't want to waste my time and be behind."

The van was starting to pull into the visitor parking lot at the school which was filling up quickly with new and returning students and their families. Julianna turned around and stared right at Roman.

"So, if you have everything figured out, what are you doing after college?"

"I..." Roman paused and stuttered, "I never said I have everything figured out! There are a couple of options. Mostly it will depend on which college I pick. I could go for law, business, the tech sector, or even political science. I'm still weighing my options and want to be fully able to choose the best path. Besides, it's better to do more than one thing and not get stuck in some rut."

"Mm." is all Julianna said with her eyebrows raised high. She turned back and took her seat belt off as they pulled into a parking spot.

Roman shoved all of his documents back into his binder and checked his appearance in the rear view mirror to make sure he was presentable. His hair was black in its immaculate crew cut that was long on the top, he straightened his collar although it was fine, and brushed imaginary dirt off of the thighs of his slacks. He walked over to his mom, gave her a hug, and said he would text her when he got done with registration. To clear his mind of all the chatter on the unexpected car ride, he walked away hurriedly. Right now focus and determination was needed so the last year of high school would go on as seamlessly as the first three had.

2 Juliet

Julianna and Valerie watched Roman go up the stairs. Valerie helped her get her bag and guitar out of the van.

"Well, this is it! Registration for your first day of high school! I know you've been here before, but it's been a while so at least let me walk you over to the new vocation building. It is state of the art and great for training in the trades or secondary education."

"Sure thing Mrs. M... I mean Val. I have the print out from online of which classes I want and should be able to figure it out well enough, but I need to get a student ID and class schedule card before registration starts."

They strolled through the milling families towards the new building. Verona High was an old campus, the first built in the city. It mostly had students whose families were alumni for three or more generations back. Kids and adults alike turned their heads to stare as Julianna passed by. At least no one was whispering or pointing. Yet.

Valerie was completely unfazed by Julianna's appearance. She knew that Angelica, Julianna's mother, had been something of a wild child through adolescence. She knew because Valerie had instigated most of their transgressions. They survived, and so had the town, and now they were both married, middle aged, respectable mothers. Angelica got to travel the world through her art and through her husband's military career. Valerie had stuck closer to home and was involved in the community. Her husband had worked in the city government before teaching at the local community and there wasn't a lot of time or money to go out on dalliances. Both Esteban and Valerie took on shifts at the family restaurant. A Cuban-American fixture since Esteban's grandparents settled in the community before he was born. It was nearly a scandal when she got pregnant with Roman.

Angelica finished school and did things in the right order. They got to have their children grow up together in a way, but the age difference and widely different personalities made it so they never were as connected as their mothers. Valerie considered Angelica more of a sister, more of family, than her own family. Julianna was Angelica's, which meant she was also Valerie's. It also was hard parenting a son that wasn't interested in any of the same things. Julianna was the closest thing she'd ever have to a daughter and she'd make sure to love and nurture her like her own.

When they got to the doors of the vocational building Julianna smiled and gave Valerie a big hug, which was kind of awkward with how much she was carrying.

"Thank you so much, Val, I'll take it from here. I'm sure that Roman is probably almost done being Mister Efficiency. Mom will pick me up on the way back from the gallery and I can hang out here until then. And I do have my cell phone if anything goes wrong."

"Oh, sure thing dear," Valerie said disappointed, but understanding, "We will see you tonight for dinner at our house. Don't hesitate to call. For anything."

Valerie walked back the way she came hoping it went smoothly. Julianna went through the glass paned doors into the already crowded building foyer. She got in line to get her card, but they weren't going to start handing them out for another hour and forty minutes. That's fine, a lot of classes would be filled up, but she would be towards the front of getting whatever class she wanted.

Every student in front of her was with at least one parent. People were nervously talking, or staring at their phones, guarding their spots like they were camping out for Black Friday shopping. Absolutely no one looked familiar. Six or seven years will do that.

More people got in line behind her. Soon the line was out the door. It was first come, first serve, and the competition hung thick in the atmosphere. She was thankful to be inside where the air condition was, instead of outside in the heat. It felt like an eternity, but the line started moving. Slowly. Julianna double checked that she had her documents in order. Military ID, updated shot record, her list of classes, and a paper confirming she was enrolled at this school. She watched the people in front of her get their check marks, picture, and then school ID to be let out to the rest of the building to sign up for their desired classes. Freshmen could only get leftovers since upperclassmen got to register first. As long as she got her electives she would be happy.

"Next!" a stern faced woman called out and Julianna shuffled forward.

"Hi here is my..."

"Last name!"

"Oh, Carpenter, I have..."

"I'll check it off," the woman said and took Julianna's papers. After some thumbing and note scratching she handed Julianna her registration card and a red slip of paper, "You can start registering down the hall now."

"Oh, I thought I took the picture for my ID first..."

"Not looking like that you don't. Read what I handed you. Fix that mess and come back before the first day of school. NEXT!"

The girl behind her started getting her things out on the counter and Julianna had to walk out the door into the main hall.

She looked at the woman's name placard before getting all the way out. Cummings. Julianna would be sure to tell her mother how she had been treated. She wouldn't have minded being told to cut her hair if it had been done politely. Now it was a matter of honor and pride. The school still hadn't forwarded the student handbook as requested. Julianna got her core classes out of the way first. English, science, math, Italian, and gymnastics were pretty close together anyhow. She needed those in specific time slots to have her schedule open for drama and guitar. Drama was a breeze, she wasn't trying to get into advanced. She made her way through the crowded hallway to the room that was set up for the music department.

Julianna leaned against the wall right inside the door to take it all in. There were tables set up for everything; choir, orchestra, steel drum, marching band, jazz band, and guitar. An older man with glasses and a school staff polo shirt sat behind the table for guitar with an older teenager who must be a class aide. There was no line, Julianna took a deep breath, and walked up to the table. The boy scowled and the man's eyes widened, but he smiled in a way that wasn't friendly at all.

"Hi, my name is Julianna, but I go by J. Just the letter. I'm almost done registering and I'd like to sign up for advanced guitar. I filled up my other slots first to be sure there would be no schedule conflicts with my core classes."

The man looked at her and stared for an uncomfortably long time before answering, "Advanced guitar? All of the younger players have turned in their letters of recommendation from their previous teacher in town months ago. Which middle school did you attend?"

"Oh, sorry, my family just moved back to town. My dad is in the military so I was home schooled the past two years and attended military schools at different bases before that. I don't have a letter because this would be my first time taking an instrument class in school, I've only had private tutors before."

With this new information the boy got the same unfriendly smile the teacher had. The two shared a look and the teacher continued.

"So sorry dear, but it wouldn't be fair to other students who earned the spot through the right channels to let you jump ahead. Beginning guitar is filled and would conflict with your schedule anyhow. I won't keep you, do you have a course book with you so you can look up another class? If not, you can head down to the counseling office in the main building and they will set you up."

Julianna stared at the man, then at the student. Other people in the room were beginning to look over, but she didn't move and she waited until the boy opened his mouth to talk to her before she spoke to cut him off.

"That's fine. I brought my own guitar in for an audition just in case."

She sat her bag on the table on top of syllabuses and pamphlets for various classes. She put her case on the floor and pulled out her black and chrome guitar. It was a gorgeous instrument, the shine gave off an almost menacing feeling as she slung the strap over her shoulder. The teacher and student were starting to protest, but she tuned them out while she tuned each string. A woman was coming over from the choir table, but it was too late to stop her as she wordlessly began to play.

She opened with <u>Barracuda</u> by Heart. Eyes closed she played completely frozen, a statue, willing with all her might that no one would try to interrupt her. Mid-way through she transferred into Jimi Hendrix and <u>Villanova Junction</u>. After a few bars she opened her eyes to see that the entire room had become frozen itself. The teacher and student were both gawking, gobsmacked, gripping the table. All eyes were on her. As she finished, she began straight into Eric Clampton's <u>Layla</u>.

She was getting more comfortable and feeling power through performing. She wasn't tired of playing, her fingers could go for ages; but her legs were aching. She stared down at the two at the table one last time with a wicked smile. She looked around the room as she played, finally. Expressions ranged from shock, to anger, to approval. As she finished <u>Layla</u> and went seamlessly into Frank Zappa's <u>Black Napkins</u> she hopped up on a counter in the back of the room, behind the hodgepodge of tables. She glanced up and the doorway was crammed with faces and there was a growing din from out in the hallway of those trying to figure out what was going on. She flowed straight into Santana's <u>Soul Sacrifice</u> and noticed some of the parents were dancing much to the embarrassment of their children. She noticed the haughty guitar teacher trying to get to the back of the room to a phone. No one was moving to make room for him. She skipped straight to the grand finale: The Runaways <u>Cherry Bomb</u>. She finished before the teacher even got to the phone. She walked over to her case and put her guitar back in firmly, took her bag off the table without disturbing any of the papers.

People were cheering and clapping once she had finished and she shouted over the noise, "Thank you, Sir, for the opportunity, but I think I'd much rather try my hand at learning steel drum and widen my instrumental skill set."

The teacher at that table already had a clipboard out for her and eagerly reached for her course schedule card.

3 Romeo

Inside of the administration office was fairly quiet. Most desks were empty and people who were there were silently working. Roman went to the counselor's office and signed in on the clipboard. He had known his class schedule since the third quarter of the previous year, but it didn't hurt to stay on top of things. Sitting in the lobby he counted the ceiling tiles to make sure there were still fifty-seven and a half in the awkward shaped room. He liked to keep time in unconventional ways. Counting tiles, visualizing someone's trip to travel to where he was, counting buses passing by on the street. It was a way to meditate without getting too deep. It wasn't long until the counselor called him back.

Ms. Sepulveda was a great counselor and always remembered who Roman was. It might have had something to do that while she only worked with students with the last names starting with L-N, she was fortunate that Roman was a Montero and most likely to be valedictorian of his class. She helped him get through the PSATs to help him qualify for the National Merit Scholar Competition, made sure he was ready for the ACT in the spring of his junior year, and she was helping him with resources for the SATs in the fall. The fact that Roman was also a star athlete of two sports also gave her lots to remember him. Unknown to him, his popularity and success was part of her job security. Roman always figured she was that bubbly and interested in all students, but he didn't realize that other students had to do a lot of the hard work of being recognized on their own. Ms. Sepulveda was nice, and good at her job, but the system is stacked against counselors and the kids who need the most help.

"Good to see you Roman, let's get right into it and see where you stand with your requirements."

"Thanks Ms. Sepulveda, I hope your summer has been restful and relaxing."

"Intelligent, athletic, and polite. I wish every student I saw was as well planned as you are. You do most of the work for me, please don't tell Principal Andrews."

They sat down in her office and she typed in his name, matric number, and date of birth. He handed her his schedule sheet and frowned as she was staring at her computer in some disbelief.

"Is the program a little slow today? I know freshmen are registering on campus today. I'm in no rush, so don't worry," Roman told her, trying to make sure she wasn't upset.

"No, no it isn't that. Not at all. I don't know how to explain this..." Ms. Sepulveda was shocked at what the computer was showing. "It seems like you are short a fine arts credit for graduation."

The uncomfortable silence filled the room for what seemed an eternity. Roman stared at Ms. Sepulveda with his mouth hanging agape. She was flipping through course schedules from years past. She held out the one from his freshman year, the year before that, and the current year.

"I took digital art freshman year. I have that credit finished, it's only one requirement. This has to be a mistake!"

"Look here. Your freshman year was the year the state dropped from requiring two fine art credits, however, you took algebra for high school credit in eighth grade and so your graduation requirements are locked in for the previous year. Thank goodness it wasn't something more drastic! You took a visual art class so that means you are required to take a performing art class."

Romeo grabbed the booklet and scanned it frantically. "No, no, no, no, no, no! This is a disaster. There has to be a loophole or some way to excuse this. Maybe I can retake algebra and be grandfathered into the same group of graduation requirements! I don't, I can't…"

Ms. Sepulveda cut him off, "Roman calm down, it will be okay. I am so sorry we didn't straighten this out long ago. There is no wiggle room, that is, if you just want to graduate without the requirements to go straight to university. Unfortunately, unless you play an instrument, there is only one class still available to fit in with your schedule and we will have to drop AP Calculus, but you have more than enough mathematics credits to have an impressive college application."

"What class is available?" Roman barely got this out, his face was down in his hands.

"First Year Theater."

"NO! No way!" Roman practically jumped out of his seat and it fell to its side.

This shocked Ms. Sepulveda who was having a difficult time remaining composed and was suddenly worried that this could cause her to lose her job, "An instrument! We could get you into marching band or perhaps steel drum?"

"I play sports, I can't be in the band and be on a team! And I don't know anything about music! I barely listen to music!"

"Right now, I have to make sure we fill that spot. I will change your schedule and will call to see if anything can be done. This is going to be my top priority. You haven't happened to do any extracurricular performance activities outside of school in the past three years have you?"

"No. No, ma'am. Academics and athletics have been my two main focuses." Roman stooped to straighten up the chair as he spoke. "I am going to speak to my family and see what we can do. I'm sorry for my behavior. This isn't your fault, I should have caught this. I should have been more careful."

"Roman, it will be alright! It's your senior year and you are a star student for our school. Just think of how many young underclassmen you can inspire by taking a class with so many opportunities. Looking into something new can be scary, but widening your knowledge is never a bad thing! We have a few more weeks until classes actually start. This isn't the end of the world."

Logically, he knew she was right. It would look good to have another art credit on his transcripts, but a little odd to have it in his senior year. Emotionally he was having a crisis of epic proportions. He didn't want to tell his mom. Or his dad. Or anyone. This was exactly the sort of thing that his mom had wanted. Him to be involved in something other than work, work, work. Freshmen? Theater geeks? It would be okay. He could work behind the scenes and be on the crew. That was it! Stage crew! He could be a grunt, just build sets, man the lights. He had experience with video and audio so maybe he could record plays and upload them for the school. He didn't have to act, it wouldn't come to that.

He reached out his hand to Ms. Sepulveda, "Thank you. I will be in touch. Please let me know if you find a way to fix this."

Roman got out of the main building and sat down heavily on the top step. He pulled out his phone and saw a message:

Mom: I'm running a few errands. Julianna has her own ride. Text when you're done.

It was hardly after nine. He had time to compartmentalize the problem. This looked a lot like sulking as he sat his phone next to him and put his face into his hands on his knees. He was so focused inward on his own misfortune that he didn't feel the presence of someone coming up behind him.

"Are you really that much of a dork that you're sad you still have a few more weeks before we come back to this drudgery?"

The voice belonged to Roman's best friend, Mercutio. They had become best friends in kindergarten and while they were younger were always the odd balls. In truth, they didn't have much in common. Mercutio would rather play around and have a good time than take a moment to consider being ambitious. He also had a smart mouth that had gotten him what must be a record number of detentions and a few suspensions along the way. Still, he was not a complete delinquent and was Roman's most trusted confidant. Mercutio sat down beside him.

"Why so glum, chum?"

"You're going to be an ass about it."

An expression of put on surprise came across Mercutio's face, "Me? Be asinine? Oh, well, that has never happened! Come on, guy, tell me what's wrong."

"My credits got screwed up."

Mercutio snorted and quickly recovered without fully cracking up, "Sorry. Sorry! What do you mean? You aren't, like, going to have to repeat a grade or anything, right?"

With a heavy sigh Roman quickly filled him in, "Since I took high school algebra in eighth grade I am locked into that year's requirements for graduation. I only took one fine arts credit so I have to take a performing art class this year or else I won't have the right credits to look at universities. Finding out now means that there is only one class other than instrumental classes still open."

"Annnnnd thaaaaat iiiiis?" Mercutio slowly waited for the big reveal.

"First Year Theater."

The noisy squeal that came out of Mercutio was barely human. Groups of people across the campus looked over in annoyance. Especially when he laughed so hard he rolled down to the bottom of the stairs.

"I TOLD YOU!" Roman yelled at him and started to walk the opposite way to the accessibility ramp and the street.

"You! In theater?! Aw man, no way. Come on. Come. ON!"

"SHUT UP!"

As Roman stormed down the ramp Mercutio ran to the bottom of it and tried to embrace him. Roman shoved him and they wrestled just a bit.

"This is great, you are going to have the best time. You know what, I'll see if I can change my schedule and get in there with you. I'll bring popcorn. We'll put it on the internet like a video diary sort of thing. "The Injustice of the Modern Educational System". What do you think?"

"I think you should shut up and I should never tell you anything! The counselor is going to try and fix it. It might not even happen."

"Okay, you were right, I'm an ass. You're the only one who puts up with me consistently. Come back to my place and we can play some games."

"I don't have time. I have things to do."

"It's your last summer before you graduate high school so no, you don't have things to do. This is the last time you don't have things to do until you retire when you're old. Plus at my house you don't have to talk to your parents. Come on."

Roman stopped and looked up at the sky, refusing to look directly at Mercutio. He had a point so he responded to his mom's message on the phone:

Roman: Going over to Mercutio's to play games. Be home later.

Mom: Sounds good. Message later if you're staying the night or if you'll come home. Love you.

Roman: Love you, too. I'll let you know.

"Aw, you're such a better son than I am." Mercutio teased, looking over Roman's shoulder.

"I thought I told you to shut up."

4 Juliet

For the entirety of the car ride home Julianna allowed her mom to dominate the conversation about her day at the gallery. Inventory, new pieces, arrangements for a new fall showcase were all things that Angelica was putting onto her plate. Being back in their hometown meant she could finally, finally put down permanent roots. Their house had been the one that Angelica had grown up in, and was given when her parents downsized to a smaller home. When Charles began tours overseas the home was lived in by Angelica's brother. His family had just moved out as they were coming back to town so it was a win-win. Julianna's dad should be home for good in September and until that time Angelica was going to become an essential part of the art scene.

When they arrived home Julianna ran straight up to her room and hopped online. She checked social media and messaged her cousin Rose who was friends with Roman and Mercutio. From down stairs she could hear her mom's phone ringing and as she finished filling in Rose on the details of how registration went Angelica began calling for her.

"JULIANNA CHASTITY CAMPBELL GET DOWN HERE NOW!"

"COMING MOM."

Julianna obeyed promptly and walked into the living room with her best practiced innocent face. "Is everything alright?"

"I just got off the phone with Principal Andrews who said that you made a scene at registration! You were disrespectful and threatening to a teacher? You haven't even started classes yet! What were you thinking?!"

"Mom, chill out, it's fine. That's not how it went down at all. Listen."

To her credit, Angelica was very good at listening and motioned for Julianna to sit down with her at the couch.

"So first I tried to take a picture for my school ID and the lady at the front desk, Mrs. Cummings, said my hair was out of dress code and I'd have to go back before classes start. I don't remember reading anything about hairstyles in the school paperwork, do you? Anyhow, she gave me my class card and I registered for all of my classes and saved guitar for last just so they couldn't tell me that there was a conflict with my schedule. When I went to the music room I tried to talk to the teacher and he said I wasn't allowed to take advanced guitar if I hadn't gone to a previous school in the district with a letter of recommendation. So I tried to show him my letters and he turned me away. I decided to give an audition."

There was a pause as Angelica stared at Julianna trying to detect any omissions.

Finally she said, "And you didn't bother mentioning that you have been in international, prestigious orchestras and even had your own solo performances in front of thousands? That you've had albums recorded for violin and piano? You didn't start with who you are or what you've done?!"

"Mom. I don't want to be treated differently for who I am, I want to be treated fairly for being like anyone else. If some self-important teacher judges me by how I look, not how I sound when I respectfully talk to them, then I don't have anything to learn from them. I shouldn't have to use clout to get some common courtesy."

"Julianna you are not to try and teach your elders a lesson, you tend to make everything so much harder on yourself. I told the principal that we will come in next week to sit down and conference with the teacher and get you into the appropriate class at your level. You were almost kicked out of school for what you pulled today! You didn't mention it to me right away because you knew you were in the wrong. The principal totally reversed his decision when he realized who you are."

"Mom, oh my god, no, you don't get it. I'm not taking guitar. I know way more than that jerk of a teacher does. I signed up for steel drum, there is nothing to fix, I don't need to talk to anyone about my classes. The teacher for steel drum was cool and not judgy. All I want is my hair and my ID. I'll call Principal Andrews and apologize if you want."

"You and your morals, you don't put up with any crap, just like your father. Oh well, I guess I should give him a call now. He wanted to hear how your day went. I'll call the school tomorrow and see what the dress code says about hair. If you have to change it, that isn't the end of the world."

"Thanks, mom." And with that Julianna ran back up stairs. Rose had bombarded her with a wall of text in the little bit she had stepped away.

Rose: You should come out tonight!

Julianna: Out? Where?

Rose: There is a teen club that has a seventeen and under night with live bands. We can go and make fun of people.

Julianna: I'll ask my mom. What time?

Rose: Eight 'til twelve.

Julianna scurried down the stairs and waved furiously at her mom on the phone with her dad. After a moment Angelica smiled and said, "Hold on a minute honey, Julianna has a question. What's up?"

"Can I go out with Rose to a club tonight? It's seventeen and under no funny business! Hi Dad! Love you!" The last part she shouted at the phone's direction.

"I suppose. Just call or text to check in every hour, understood?"

Julianna ran over to her mother and gave her an awkward hug and cheek kiss, "Thanks, Ma." She then bounded back upstairs.

Julianna: S'all good. I'm gunna get ready!

Rose: I'll be there quarter 'til eight.

5 Romeo

No one was at Mercutio's house as they pulled into the driveway. The boys got out of the car and went straight to the kitchen for snacks and drinks which they took down to the game room. Mercutio put some music on the computer that was under the stairs. There was a table for eight surrounded by bookshelves of board games, tabletop role playing games, bowls of multi-sided dice, miniatures, and boxes of all kinds of cards. Past the table was a couch, some mismatched dining chairs and barstools, and a few gaming chairs with a bean bag. The TV across from the couch was older, but hooked up with various game systems and was in the middle of two bookshelves containing movies and games. Mercutio loaded up a first person shooter and they played for a while talking without really saying anything.

"Hey, how come you were at school today anyhow?" Roman finally thought to ask.

"It was freshman registration, I ran the GSA table in the small auditorium for clubs to make sure kids know what resources are available to them. Not every middle school is as open as our high school is and our high school isn't as welcoming as it could be."

Mercutio had come out to Roman when they were in sixth grade. He came out to his family shortly after that, and to everyone in seventh grade. Roman had joined the Gay Straight Alliance club with Mercutio for support that year and never had much of a hassle from any kids. Mercutio's brother was younger and was smaller, he had been jumped a few times by kids who were too scared of Mercutio or Roman to mess with them out right, but could easily take it out on Sloane for having a gay, older brother. Sloane was three years younger and was going to be a sophomore, being at the same school as Mercutio had alleviated a lot of the issues and it helped that as kids got older they were gradually more understanding of differences and less hateful.

"That's cool, I didn't realize they even set up booths for clubs this early."

"I talked with student counsel about it last year and they thought it'd be a good way to give new students options to consider before clubs are finalized in September. Plus this way I get to see if there are any cute underclassmen before anyone else." The last part he said with a big grin as Roman punched him in the ribs.

"You're a little old for a freshman, don't you think?"

"What I think is that you are not someone in the position to be giving me dating advice with your limited experience and unwillingness to date me."

"I have experience..." Roman weakly started to defend himself. He totally ignored the jab about dating Mercutio, because it was out of the question since they had been friends for so long. Also, Mercutio repeatedly let Roman know how he was so not his type.

Mercutio just scoffed and swapped his weapons out for something that lent itself to sniping more than melee.

"I do! Don't scoff at me!"

"Name one person you've gone out with. One."

"Well last year I took Rose to junior prom."

"Rose! That doesn't count, not even close, she said she tried to kiss you at the end of the night and you shook her hand. Shook. Her. Hand. Come on, man!"

"Dating just isn't interesting to me! That doesn't mean that I can't tell you that dating a freshman would be a bad idea."

"Maybe there will be a new student or freshman that will change your mind this year. Someone to break through your impenetrable wall, Romulus, as long as they stay impregnable, if you need protection I can help you out."

"Ugh, you are so gross, that is the furthest thing from my mind."

The door from upstairs opened and swung shut as Sloane came down the steps. He had grown a bit since last year and had come into his own through drama and being active in the local SCA group that recreated medieval European culture. He walked behind the couch and plopped down on the beanbag.

"Hey Sloane." Both Roman and Mercutio said in unison with the same monotone inflection.

"Hey."

The older boys kept playing and were doing better at some PVP until they came across a higher powered group. Sloane kept typing away at his phone. Music played softly from the computer in the corner.

"Hey. There is a thing tonight." Sloane said suddenly, breaking the stillness.

"A thing." Roman repeated, not looking away from the TV, but raising his eyebrow.

"At the Library. Thirteen to seventeen only with some chaperones and live music. Buncha local bands showing off and some first time sets. We should go, you guys will go with me, right? I don't want to go alone."

Roman and Mercutio finished up their round and got their phones out so they could read the details for themselves. A lot of people seemed to be going, looked like it was going to be alright.

"I'll go with you, how about it, Roman? You want to check it out or are you going to ditch us brothers for an exciting night with your textbooks?"

"Actually, this sounds alright. Nothing wrong checking it out tonight. Let me text my mom."

Roman: Hey mom. Going to stay overnight at Mer's. Going to the Library for a while then will come back here. That alright?

Mom: As long as you guys stay together that's fine. Text or call if you need anything or if anything changes. Love you.

Roman: Love you, too.

"Alright! Let's go get some pizza on the way!" Sloane was suddenly energized and bounded up the stairs in about three steps. The older boys followed him up slowly, still checking their phones. They got into the car and drove to the pizza place by the Library. The Library was an inclusive club that had been in the city for generations. It was named so young people could go to hang out and honestly tell their parents they were going to the library. Parents who grew up in town knew what was up and were almost universally accepting of their kids going there to hang out. It was a rite of passage and cultural touchstone for the teens and young adults of the city.

The boys got an extra large pepperoni pizza to share and some drinks. Sloane flipped through his phone and nudged Mercutio next to him, "Dude check this out!"

He flipped his phone around so Roman and Mercutio could watch. It was a video of the end of Julianna's "audition" for guitar that morning. It had gone completely viral across all social media platforms.

"Holy shit, Mr. DeSalvo looks like he is going to implode! Who is that chick?" Mercutio gasped, wonderstruck.

"Julianna." Roman said with solid annoyance. How could she decide to be that outrageous and disrespectful? This was going to bring a ton of unwanted attention to her, she might get kicked out of school before the first day. Was there a precedent for that?

"What?!" Mercutio and Sloane shot looks up at Roman in disbelief.

"No, Julianna is the tiny, meek, annoying little brat. This here is a young woman of indisputable boldness. How do you know? It can't be her!"

With the news that his meticulously planned out schedule was in threat Roman had totally forgotten that Julianna was back in town. It had been jarring to see her transformation, but he probably still wouldn't have thought to bring it up to Mercutio. They had met through the years, but were never especially close. Roman didn't think it was that important, but now life was going to be more complicated.

"Her dad is retiring and she just moved back with her mom. They're settling down and going to stay here. My mom drove her to registration today since I was going in to meet my counselor and apparently she is completely unhinged. Nobody messes with DeSalvo!"

"You already saw her? Before this happened?! And you didn't think to mention it? Roman you are the worst at gossip, hold on I am going to message Rose."

Mercutio started typing furiously while ripping bites out of his pizza. Sloane was sitting and staring at his phone completely in awe. He had started in beginning guitar the year before, but transferred out because Mr. DeSalvo made him uncomfortable. The teacher never did anything that he could actually report him for, but he could tell that he was treated differently and graded unfairly. He wasn't learning anything because Mr. DeSalvo spent all of his time with the students who really showed promise, the ones who weren't from unconventional families. Basically, if the students already knew how to play a guitar he was nice to them, but any student that was there to learn everything they weren't worth the bother. It worked out for Sloane, because he was able to get into drama and realized he had a knack for lighting and audio visual tech. The added bonus was he didn't have to put up with a power hungry, tyrannical teacher for an entire year. Students in guitar either bought into his ego or dropped the class soon after starting it.

"Dude! They're already there! Inside!" Mercutio waved his phone at Roman.

"Big deal, hopefully Rose can keep her from being a complete maniac. She isn't performing tonight, is she?"

"No, looks like a few new groups and Tyler's band with some karaoke at the end."

"Maybe I should just go home, you guys can have a good time without me. I don't want to see Julianna, Rose, or Tyler. I just want to wallow in self pity without dealing with a ton of jerks."

"Rose isn't a jerk, she's cool! Besides, do you want to go home and explain to your mom that you're at home early because you don't want to see Julianna AND about your credit conflict?" Mercutio got very defensive. Rose was his other best friend since eighth grade. Roman had stayed in GSA through seventh, but was doing too many sports through eighth. The three had met in seventh and Rose and Mercutio hung out when Roman was busy. Tyler was Rose's older brother who had graduated two years ago. He and his friends were the few kids who were cruel to Mercutio and Roman. Tyler resented that his sister was accepting of various life styles and openly friended Mercutio and he resented Roman for being more athletic, yet younger. High school became infinitely better for everyone with him out of the picture.

"Schedule conflict? What schedule conflict?" Sloane looked confused and really didn't want Roman to leave, he liked when he spent time with them like this, it reminded him of when they were all younger.

"Thanks Mercutio," Roman snapped sarcastically, "I might have to take first year drama."

"No way?! That's great! I'm retaking it to find out what I missed from first quarter last year! We'll be in a class together and I didn't think I'd ever get the chance to take a class with either of you!" Sloane was absolutely beaming.

"Sorry, Sloane, I'm not going to take it if I can absolutely help it. They messed up my course schedule and I'm trying to get it fixed," as Roman spoke anyone could see the wind being taken right out of Sloane's sails, "However, if I am going to be forced to take an unexpected class it comforts me to know I'll be in good company."

Sloane smiled softly, he knew Roman was saving his feelings. That's what made everyone love Roman, he was unequivocally kind. Well, almost everyone. The boys gathered up their garbage and started heading for the Library across the parking lot. They were let in by the security guard who ran through the rules quickly and waved them through. Inside were tables, a stage for performances or kareoke, a dance floor, pool tables, darts, and a snack bar in the back. There were also board games and cards that could be used. Sometimes card tournaments or video game parties were held at the Library. Mercutio led the way to a table next to some of his friends in GSA and the groups merged into a larger clump of adolescents.

Not long after Julianna and Rose came in and met up with the group. They pulled over another table with more chairs and started talking with a couple of kids in the GSA. Sloane was bashfully looking over, while Mercutio was playing at being aloof. Roman had gotten into a game of dominos with a couple friends. The first band was playing and kids were dancing, everyone was having fun. After a respectable amount of time Mercutio finally got over to Rose and Julianna to talk to them. Sloane looked mortified and was shaking his head at his brother and then leaned back to hide behind people. Roman doubled down on his domino focus.

"Rose! How is it going? Who is this lovely flower you are accompanied by this evening?"

"Mer!" Rose exclaimed as she reached up and hugged him. "I'm so glad you're out tonight. You remember my baby cousin Julianna? Her family is moving back to town and she starts ninth grade this year."

Julianna waved a little wave at Mercutio and said, "Call me J! I remember you, but it's been too long of a time."

Mercutio took her waving hand and shook it earnestly, "Oh you are one that is hard to forget, but it looks like you have had a transformation since last we met."

Julianna smiled coyly, but her smile suddenly turned crestfallen. Rose and Mercutio looked behind them and saw Tyler sauntering up with a few of his bandmates.

"Look at who is here! Better watch out, Jules, you should know Rose is a bad influence and has a terrible taste in friends." Tyler wedged himself in between Mercutio and Rose. Mercutio instinctively recoiled a step back.

"What are you doing here, you're old, Tyler, and don't call me Jules." Julianna fumed. She was as much of a Tyler fan as anyone else it seemed.

"I'll call you whatever I feel like and if you don't watch out you'll wind up a hag just like my sister here." Tyler grabbed Rose by the shoulders and she punched at him until he backed off laughing, "I work here as a chaperone, and play here with my band. Being so successful I like to give back to the community. Someday you might be as fortunate as me, inspiring youth and being a respectable member of society. Well, unless you continue to choose to socialize with such low class characters like my sister does."

"Better to be low class than a total creep that only has friends he has to pay to like him." Mercutio nodded back at his two band mates who were there as physical support, but weren't going to get involved.

"Shut up, Merqueertio, I'm talking to my cousin, not you!" Tyler walked across the table towards Julianna and Roman stood up to stand in front of Mercutio. "Listen, I don't know what all this nonsense is, but I heard what you pulled today at your registration. You really shot yourself in the foot causing problems with Mr. DeSalvo. If there is one man you should be working to please right now it's him. He actually has the power to help you use your talent in life and you could go pretty far. For a woman."

Tyler looked down at Julianna who slowly stood up and moved around Roman. Tyler towered over her, grinning sadistically. Sloane had scooted over and around to take Roman's spot.

"I don't need to please anyone in this life except myself. I have more talent in my eyebrow than you have in your entire body or soul. In fact, every person at this table is more talented than you in some way, because they actually have a personality and aren't devoid of common courtesy. I swear, Rose, I have always been skeptical that we're related to this insecure piece of..." is all that Julianna got out as Tyler put his hand over her face and shoved her back into her seat. Everyone stood up and started to yell, but the first band had broken set and Tyler's friends were walking over to the stage. He sneered as he turned away from them.

"ASSHOLE!" Julianna yelled after him, but they ignored her.

"Are you okay?" Sloane had come out of where he had been hiding and was kneeling next to Julianna.

"I'm... fine. I just hate how he thinks he is just better than anyone else on the planet. I'd talk to my aunt, but it just causes more problems."

"Let's get out of here. I don't want to listen to this garbage." Rose stood up and got her purse.

"Sorry guys, see you at school." Julianna winked towards Roman, Sloane, and Mercutio as they walked away, "Rose you can stay over tonight, I'll ask mom."

The rest of the kids went over to the pool tables, away from the main stage. For the most part they were able to banter, gossip, and make fun of how sad Tyler's band really was.

6 Juliet

The weekend passed uneventfully. Julianna and Rose reconnected and spent time planning when to hang out at school. Rose also volunteered to drive Julianna to school. Summer was ending quickly. By Monday it was time to go back to the school and smooth things over after the registration excitement.

"Thank you Mrs. Cummings, I'll think of you every time I need to use my student ID. I love it." Julianna practically sang to the receptionist. Her mom was completely oblivious to the undertone. A man suddenly walked through a side door and hurried towards them before Mrs. Cummings could respond.

"Mrs. Carpenter? Ms. Carpenter? I'm Mr. Andrews, what a pleasure it is to meet both of you in person. Please, come into my office."

Julianna looked around at the modest office with a few framed diplomas, family photos, a few pieces of sports memorabilia. They sat down and politely declined the water they were offered.

"Thank you for seeing us Mr. Andrews. I am thankful you've decided to give Julianna a second chance."

"Oh it's nothing, I understand how stressful it can be being a teenager. Nevermind one who has had to move around so much and is so vastly talented from such a young age. It's the most fun anyone has had at registration in a long time."

"Sorry Mr. Andrews. I really thought that the gentleman, Mr. DeSalvo, was it? Needed a demonstration of my skill set. It was standard for many of the music schools and orchestras I have toured with. I didn't mean to offend."

"None taken, and don't worry about Mr. DeSalvo. He knew it was all in good fun. We're honored that you have chosen our school and will not burden your creativity. This is what Verona High needs at a time like this. Successful young leaders shaking up the day. I've also reviewed the student dress code and code of conduct with Mrs. Cummings so she will be more sensitive to how our students choose to express themselves. Julianna, I want you to know my door is always open. If you need me, come talk to me. Join some clubs, get involved with some school activities, and have fun when school starts."

As Mr. Andrews finished Julianna looked over at the closed door and back at her new principal and smiled.

"Thank you, sir, I appreciate it. What a lucky student body this school has with a principal who is deeply interested in the happiness of all of them." Julianna was going to add something about not just the ones that have fame following them, but her mother shot her a look.

They said their goodbyes and got back to the car. Angelica had to get back to work at the gallery and dropped Julianna off at Rose's house. In her room they chose between different fighting games to play together.

"Tyler is coming over to help dad in the garage at three so we should go out somewhere."

"Alright. You know where we should go? We should get our hair cut before school starts."

Rose stopped playing and leaned over to look at Julianna, "J, you want to go cut your hair? You just made a big stink to get your hair on your student ID. Why cut it?"

"It's symbolic of starting over as a new person. Every time I see my old ID I'll remember me from before this school year. Anyone who looks close will remember I'm fierce, but I don't want to stick out if I don't have to. Besides," Julianna took the opportunity of distracting Rose to win the fight, "It's not fun if I'm allowed to have crazy hair and this way any other kid can't be pushed around by Mrs. Cummings. Plus, I guarantee she won't recognize me for at least the first quarter. It's like being a spy in disguise. I want to have all of the secret identities because being just one person can get a little dull."

Rose sat the controller up on her shelf, "You think about things way too hard, J. It's just hair! No one cares if it's spiked, dyed, or completely basic."

"You say that because your hair is completely basic. We should get you an undercut, oooh, or how about neon highlights?" Julianna was teasing, mostly, because Rose was super protective of her hair. It was long, black, straight, and beautiful. No bangs, no dye, and never shorter than her elbows. It was her own kind of rebellion because her parents would like her to have a shorter, bobbed haircut.

"Stay away from my head you hair zombie!" Rose picked up a hand mirror in feigned defense. Julianna laughed and turned the TV off.

The girls headed downstairs and climbed into the car. At the salon there was a little bit of a wait and the hairdressers raised their eyes to the girls, but kept any comments to themselves. Together the cousins flipped through style books until Julianna found what she wanted. The stylist was able to even out her sides, re-dye her hair so she had natural highlights, no more purple. The end result was a stacked bob, with some loose curls for extra body. She bought several kinds of mousse, a round brush, and some shampoo.

"You sure you don't want to reinvent yourself today?" Julianna grinned wickedly at Rose as she paid for everything.

"Positive. Hair this sexy takes a lot of work, patience, and dedication. I'm not doing anything to ruin it now! It's my senior year and I could take my pictures as Lady Godiva and get away with it!"

"Fair enough, but I really think you should get someone to do that photoshoot. I mean, there are a lot of people who would be ready to pay good money for a calendar. Could pay for your first year of college tuition."

The stylist thanked them, but gave them both a double glance not sure if they were teasing or serious. With the haircut out of the way and still a lot of time to kill they went over to the mall to walk around. All the same stores with all of the same merchandise nobody really needs. The girls found a spot in the food court to snack and people watch. Not too long after they sat down Rose recognized a girl and waved her over.

"J this is Bethany, Bethany this is J or Julianna, my cousin. She will be a freshman this year, too." Rose handled the introduction seamlessly as the girls waved to each other, "I know Bethany through swim team. I was her swim instructor a few summers back."

"Nice to meet you, do you have your schedule? I can see if we have the same lunch."

Julianna dug around in her bag to find a copy of her schedule and handed it over. Bethany had flipped her phone open and to one of the videos of J's performance at registration.

"Did you see this? Some crazy punk girl started playing in the middle of the music classes! I am so mad I missed that, I was stuck trying to get social studies to work with auto shop."

Rose put her face in her hands in a double facepalm, Julianna was grinning stupidly at Bethany. Incognito challenge accepted.

"No, I hadn't seen the video yet, but we heard about it the other night at the Library. Were you there?" Julianna pressed her hand on Rose's knee to let her know to not let on.

"No, I had to babysit that night, but I heard that Tyler's band was really off key. They went out after to another bar and got kicked out for hassling a girl. I'm so glad he won't be coaching for swim team this year. He is so demotivating."

The subtext of creepy was very easy to pick up on from Bethany's tone. It looked like they had the same teachers for math and drama, but different lunches. They exchanged phone numbers and social media handles and went on their way.

Nothing Julianna did phased Angelica anymore. She trusted her daughter enough to not do anything dangerous. Julianna wasn't interested in serious dating, terrified of not being in control, and had better judgment than most adults. Still, she couldn't understand all of the things her daughter did and just accepted them as they came up. A more controlling mother would have been thrilled to see a more subdued haircut, Angelica just admired how mature the hair made her little girl look.

It was three more months until Charles would be discharged and home for good. He also supported Julianna's individuality without being overly indulgent. He had seen too many places and known too many people to really worry about how people looked as long as they carried themselves with dignity, respect, and kindness. As a dad he was immensely proud of his daughter, but he would rather have her be happy and kind first, smart and talented second.

The first day of high school would be here shortly and everything was in place. A few friends, classes set, and the motivation to accept any challenges.

7 Romeo

Roman was staring as if he could stare through the mirror. His schedule was non-negotiable, that is, unless he wanted to take a class during summer school. That wasn't an option if he wanted any real colleges to take his admission paperwork seriously.

He brushed his teeth, flossed, and rinsed with mouthwash. Roman had shaved, moisturized, applied appropriate amounts of deodorant and cologne. Perfect grades, athletic prowess, a kind and gentle personality, and great hygiene practices made Roman very popular with girls, but he still hasn't had a real relationship. This chagrined his mother to no end. While she did not want her son to grow up too quickly, she wanted to find him a partner and companion. She didn't want grandchildren, not yet, but she had looked forward to him having someone to go on dates with.

None of that frivolousness was appealing to Roman. He wanted solitary independence with no distractions from his ambitions. His interests were almost diametrically opposed to those of his mother. She had never been one to keep her grades up, nor had she been a jock. Finding a party and having a good time had been her primary focuses in her adolescence. She wanted better for her son, but she also wanted him to be happy and have fun before he grew too old.

Valerie had made a special first day of school breakfast with eggs, home fries, bacon, and some salsa. Roman served himself with a glass of orange juice and a mug of coffee. His dad was reading the news on his phone and taking some notes on a pad of paper. Roman's mom sat down in between them at the table.

"So tonight we are going to have Angelica and Julianna over for dinner so you both have to be home on time." Valerie stared to make sure they both heard her.

"Yes, dear, I'll be home on time. My department is just having some last minute organizational meetings about last minute class changes." Roman's father, Esteban, was a professor at the local community college. He taught political science and history classes. He got a little obsessive about finding current events to frame lessons around and was constantly tweaking and changing his content to stay relevant. As a tenured professor he worked harder than would be expected as a lot of teachers figure out a formula that works for them and keep the same class format for years.

When Esteban was younger he had been in a band and had worked for his dad's contractor business, mom's restaurant, and from time to time would help an uncle at his auto shop. He worked a lot of odd jobs while going through college himself and had dabbled in local government. As a young father he wanted to be sure his son wouldn't have to work as hard to get a start in life, but never regretted all of his experiences and hard work. He was a great dad and supportive husband, but completely laid back where his wife was much more of a helicopter parent.

"Roman?" Valerie hadn't gotten a confirmation from her son.

"Yeah?"

"You'll be home in a timely manner?"

"Yes, Mom, don't worry. No practice or meetings. Just a straightforward, syllabus filled, first day."

"Perfect. Watch out for Julianna and be helpful. Starting high school can be scary, especially for a girl who has had such a hard time moving from place to place. You are the only person she will know."

"I am not going to go out of my way to find her, Mom. I've got my own stuff to do and I'm not a babysitter. She will be fine, she knows Rose and has been taking care of herself."

"But it's so good to have a girl around. When people see she's friends with you that will make her social life so much easier. You have a responsibility as a community leader to support such a good family friend. Esteban, tell him it's important to reach out to a girl like Julianna."

"Listen to your mother, son. Valerie, you could also tone it down a notch, I think Julianna will be just fine without making Roman be a guardian angel. It's just high school. They make it foolproof nowadays where you just follow all the other kids around and figure it out."

"I just want my best friend's daughter to feel a warm welcome! Is that so hard for you both to understand?" Valerie grabbed all their plates and loaded the dishwasher huffily, "I'll be waiting in the van for you Roman."

Roman and Esteban shared glances. It was easier to let Valerie feel like she was controlling all of the situations than try to help her with anything. Roman would let his mom know if he saw Julianna, but wouldn't make it a top priority. The last thing he needed was for a freshman weirdo to go all doe eyed and get infatuated with him.

Roman's mom dropped him off early so there weren't any crowds yet. He went straight to his first class and spent a large chunk of time organizing his planner and making sure he had his first quarter schedule tight. Lunch was uneventful, he didn't run into Mercutio at all, and he headed to the dreaded theater room for drama class. The teacher, Mr. Henderson, was a really dedicated educator and facilitated the student council with a history teacher in addition to running a fantastic drama program. Roman had met him off and on through Rose and Mercutio through the years.

"THE BELL HAS NOT YET RUNG!" a voice bellowed as Mr. Henderson came out from his office slash tech booth holding a microwave burrito. His face brightened when he saw it was just Roman entering the little theater.

"Roman! What a surprise, I read my class list and saw your name. I've got to say I'm not disappointed. We're going to have some great plays this year."

"Sorry to interrupt your lunch time. I like to get to classes early to find a good seat. I think I'll just grab one back here to be out of the way and get a good spot for observing. I'm ready to learn all about stagecraft and the magic behind the scenes." Roman was already claiming a spot as he spoke in the back row so he could also make an easy escape.

Mr. Henderson just considered him curiously. He had been teaching long enough, and had seen enough kids, to know what would be their best place in the theater. It had to come internally from the student's mind, though, and forcing someone to do something they weren't comfortable with always would backfire. He knew Roman wasn't the type to have stage fright, he was actually a confident public speaker. Time would tell if he actually had any acting talent.

"Well, whatever happens, I'm happy to have you aboard and hope you at least have a little fun." and with that Mr. Henderson went back into the tech booth to prepare for class.

The bell rang not long after and kids started filtering in. It was almost totally freshman and with Roman sitting in the back, most nervously sat down quietly, shooting glances as if they were wondering if this was the teacher. Sloane came in calmly, until he spotted Roman and bounded over like an excited puppy to sit next to him. They made small talk and checked out a few of the students around. As the warning bell rang Rose walked in with two other girls. They made a beeline for the front row and didn't even notice anyone else in the room because they were busy chatting. As the final bell rang Mr. Henderson greeted the class.

"Welcome, all of you, to beginning theater. I know most of you would assume this is a freshman class, but we have students of all grades here. Some have more theater experience than others. You will be asked to do things that might make you uncomfortable, but you will never be embarrassed or have your dignity hurt. This is a fun, safe, and welcoming classroom. I have very few students in my advanced theater classes this year and they are working on their own special projects. Some have been working in the community volunteering for drama clubs for younger children or interning at local theaters. If you enjoy this year you may be taking their places in the years to come!"

Roman fidgeted a little in his seat, it was a good opening lecture, but where was the syllabus? What assignments were required? How hard was it going to be to maintain his GPA? Part of him wanted to do the bare minimum, but the other half needed to excel. Mr. Henderson began to take attendance.

"When I say your name, please correct me if I say it wrong. And don't stop correcting me until I say it right. Oh, and if you have a name you'd rather be called by, please let me know."

Flipping through a notebook Roman started to write out his own syllabus and Cornell note page to have something to study from this class.

"Julianna Carpenter?"

The tip of Roman's pencil snapped.

"Here! And I just go by "J" thanks."

"Not a problem," Mr. Henderson spoke as he scratched out her name and wrote J above it, "Welcome to class. Rose Tran?"

"Here."

A hand grasped Roman's shoulder. He had been dumbfounded and was trying to put together the events that had just happened. Rose he had seen, but Julianna wasn't *here,* not a chance. His choice of sitting in the back had completely backfired and he couldn't see who was pretending to be Julianna. That juvenile delinquent was going to make this year even worse than being stuck in a drama class.

"...here..." Sloane squeaked out, still grasping onto Roman's shoulder.

"Good to see you, Sloane! Hope you had a good summer, look forward to starting off right this year."

"Sh... Ju... Jay... She's *in our class*!" Sloane barely breathed this to Roman.

Roman pulled out a pen and wrote:

No she isn't, not today, that's not her.

I know her voice! That was her!

No way, that girl is normal!

Sloane stared at the paper and frowned and looked back up to Roman confused and hurt. Roman turned and stared hard at the back of the girls' heads by Rose. Shit. That was her, but masquerading as a typical girl. This meant that Roman would have to "check in" after class to keep his word to his mom.

"Roman, I saw you earlier, are you alright?" Mr. Henderson was waiting for him to respond.

"Here! Here, sir, sorry I was taking notes and got lost in thought."

Some of the kids snickered and Roman thought he heard someone say, "Who needs notes from attendance? Stalker much?"

Mr. Henderson must not have heard because he finished up attendance, sent it on the computer, and went right into the lesson for the day.

"Alright, I'm going to have Bethany here hand out an envelope to every other person. Do not open the envelope, but wait for instructions."

Bethany walked around and handed an envelope accordingly. She walked up the aisle and handed one to Sloane and kept one for herself.

"In here we are going to have a short improv activity as an ice breaker. If you have an envelope, you are partnered with the person to your right," Sloane glanced at Roman and smiled as Mr. Henderson spoke, "But if you are to the left of someone with an envelope, you have to go find someone in the room to work with that you aren't in the same row as and create a triad. Don't open the envelope but on my signal, go find someone new to work with. Ready... go!"

Julianna was sitting to the left of Bethany. Sloane started stomping on Roman's foot and kicking his shin. His face had lost its color and he was gasping like a fish. Julianna had been too slow to get with any groups close by. Her gaze steadily moved to the back of the room and locked onto Sloane and Roman.

"No, no, no, aah, no, no," Sloane was nearly hypervenelating and threw himself to the floor.

Roman stared at him, shocked and wondering if he had lost his mind. He wasn't thrilled about working with Julianna, either, but he wasn't going to throw a fit about it. Julianna reached the row and stared down at the boys for the first time in ages. She was wearing a cute, pink, spaghetti strap top with a sheer blouse over it. The blouse had a pattern of pastel flowers and she had a modest skirt just to her knee and some simple, cork sandals. Her hair was neatly styled in curls and was nowhere near the trainwreck it had been only days before. Her quizzical expression turned into a smirk as she addressed them.

"Hey guys, is it okay if I work with you, or is this a private group?" She moved back to the row in front of the boys and kneeled facing them.

"Of course, no problem at all." Roman said, smiling charmingly.

"Ye.. no.. I mean I..." Sloane was now sitting on the floor, reverting his gaze from Julianna as he tried to answer. Roman and Julianna just shrugged. A loud clap from Mr. Henderson drew their attention back to the front of the room.

"Now! We're going to have a little bit of improv today. There are three slips of paper in the envelope with a suggestion, the person with the envelope will act out the scene without saying what the suggested word is. The other two have to guess what the word was on a piece of paper, I will be collecting these to grade. The person who is closest gets a point and there might be a prize for the group with the most correct guesses over all."

The convulsions bothering Sloane seemed to stop once he was given a job to do. He felt around for a slip of paper and smiled as he read it. He jumped over the back of the row of chairs and began to act out his word.

"YARG ME HEARTIES! We be setting sail on the high seas. Going to plunder and pillage some fine booty!"

He stomped back and forth with a limp as though he had a peg leg, closed one eye like he had an eye patch, and his finger bent like a hook. Roman quickly wrote "Pirate" on his paper.

"So what'd you guys put down? Oooh so close, the word was actually "swashbuckler"!" Sloane said.

"What? No way give me that." Roman wrestled to get the slip of paper that clearly said "Pirate" on it.

"Dang! That worked on some kids in a different game last year, you're too smart, Roman." Julianna started laughing as Sloane talked. He instantly turned bright red and passed the envelope over.

Roman took it from him and pulled out a paper that said "motorcycle". "Motorcycle"? He'd give it a try. He stood up behind the rows and threw his leg over an invisible motorcycle and pantomimed kicking it started while making engine revving noises. He checked his imaginary helmet and mirrors, before kicking the stand off and pretending to ride a motorcycle around. Sloane and Julianna were in absolute hysterics. He stopped, a little miffed at being laughed at. He stomped over to check their papers.

"Sorry, not motorcycle, it was "biker gang"."

It was Sloane's turn to wrestle the slip back and catch him at the lie, "Roman! And what the hell was that? You're not supposed to be a mime, you need to talk it out. It will be easier with other people when we do an interactive scene."

Roman wasn't too sure. He reached over and handed the envelope to Juliana. She read the paper thoughtfully and thoroughly. She just stood before the boys and was silent for a moment. Just when Roman was about to ask her if everything was alright she spoke.

"All the world's a stage, and all the men and women are merely players; they have their exits and their entrances, and one man in his time plays many parts, his acts being seven ages."

This dumbfounded both Sloane and Roman. They wrote something quickly and she came over and checked their papers.

"Oooh sorry, the correct answer wasn't "theater", it was "existential crisis". She smiled coyly as she said it.

The boys just stared. Sloane was mesmerized by her anytime she spoke. Roman was still trying to process her transformation and the fact that she had something of substance in her rebellious mind. He began to mark his answer wrong, but Julianna ripped his pencil away.

"You guys aren't even going to call on me? I thought that was part of the fun. This wasn't very hard to guess, or maybe we're just that good. We all tied and that means we have six out of six, I hope this isn't one of those "Everyone's a winner" games." She went back to her seat in front of them and they saw that some groups were still trying to figure out the instructions and arguing, some were frustrated and couldn't seem to act out the words, while a few were blowing it off completely.

"Show of fingers of how many more minutes each group needs? Zero? Two? Two? One? Let's go with a minute and a half and we'll regroup." Mr. Henderson checked his watch as the groups scrambled to finish and finally said very quietly, "Oedipus."

The class stared, and some whispered, "What?", except for Sloane who quietly said "Rex".

"Oedipus." Mr. Henderson barely whispered.

"Rex." This time, Julianna and Roman both responded with Sloane.

"Oedipus." Mr. Henderson said one more time.

"Rex?" chimed back almost half of the confused class.

"That is an attention getter. I don't want to lose my voice and none of you should, either. They are all theater related and I'll be watching to see who catches on quick. Good thing for Sloane is that he took half this class last year and will know a few of them. Everyone will have to be awfully quick to beat him. Let's go ahead and start with your group, Sloane, how many points did you earn as a group?"

Sloane glanced at Roman and Julianna before answering, "Six, sir."

Mr. Henderson beamed, "Six! Fantastic! I'm sure you were able to demonstrate to them how it's done. Can any group match six?"

Everyone else shook their heads and it was clear few had even finished the task.

"Come on up here all three of you. I have Sloane, Roman, and don't tell me," Mr. Henderson shut his eyes and tapped his foot while he thought, "J, wasn't it? Yes. Alright class, the prize for winning our first improv challenge is to meld all of your words into one performance and to get the answer of which words they had. Come up on stage and let's go."

Roman was in full panic mode. He was trying to logically and systematically put together a way that "theater" "motorcycle" and "pirate" would fit together. The lights on the stage were bright and he felt like he was starting to sweat when he heard Julianna's voice.

"Good evening distinguished guests. I do hope that you enjoy the following original performance in this here building that was created to perform plays. Like an amphitheater of old. This will be the location of where the drama unfolds." She stepped back with an exaggerated bow and shot looks at both boys.

"YARG! I be Fairbeard the Terrible and I have heard tell of a mystical mechanical horse!" Sloane aggressively approached Roman.

"Stop right there!" Roman's mind was racing, trying to piece together what he needed to do to fit in his part. "You will not have my, uh, hog! Away!" Roman hopped on his "motorcycle" in high speed and made the sound effects as Sloane chased him arging and yarging the whole time. The entire class was howling with laughter. Roman was out of breath and laughing, too. Sloane took his hand and Julianna took his other one. They raised their arms and bowed for the class to raucous applause.

"Wow! Masterfully done! All three of you! I wish I had recorded that as an example for my future classes. That is by far the best first day performance I have been blessed with orchestrating. However, who in the audience knew what was happening?"

Shouts of "motorcycle" and "pirate" were caught by everyone, but had they caught how Julianna fit into everything. She actually looked a little worried to Roman. A quiet voice from the front said, "Theater?"

Mr. Henderson cheered Bethany's answer and congratulated the class altogether. It was at this point he handed out the syllabus Roman had so desperately desired and explained a little bit about the course load. There would be different improv lessons, monologues, creative writing, and homework based off of the text. The largest part of the grade would include participation in the spring play which was listed as "To be announced". Tryouts for parts would be right before Thanksgiving break. A few kids asked what the play would be and all Mr. Henderson would say was, "I attended a script writing seminar over the summer and had the opportunity to modify a story to be suitable for a high school setting."

Julianna had gone back to sit with Rose and Bethany. Roman mumbled something about seeing her later and to just ask if she needed anything. Sloane was already back up in his seat by Roman.

"Having to do more work in class as a reward?" Roman said to Mr. Henderson on his climb up, "Not the best way to motivate me for next time."

Mr. Henderson was still just laughing as the bell rang and the class shuffled out to finish the afternoon.

8 Juliet

High school was fantastic. She talked her mom's ear off the entire ride home and bounded straight upstairs to add new people on her social media accounts. After a little chatting and homework she came down stairs.

"Are you ready?" Angelica had gotten a little dressed up with jewelry and a new dress.

"Yeah, Mom, why are you all fancy? We're just going over to the Montero's for dinner."

"I haven't had an excuse to dress up for so long. It will be nice to have a little dinner party. It makes me glad that you lucked out and have Roman in your theater class!"

"Really? It's not that big of a deal. He's kind of boring."

"I think he is sweet, just a little shy. You know he still isn't dating? I bet he is scared of girls, you should take him under your wing to make sure he can get more comfortable around them. You always loved playing with him when you were little. I worry about if he is depressed and covering up for it by working so hard in school."

"Mom, he's fine. He went to prom with Rose and was just super weird. He's a nice guy, but extremely two dimensional. Personally, I think he is either an android or an alien pod person sent here to learn more about our simple human lives!" Julianna made exaggerated facial expressions and wiggled her fingers by her face for effect.

"Julianna! You will be kind to that poor boy, I think he might have a crush on you and I think it'd be perfect if you were able to find a good boy to date." Angelica was standing with her hands on her hips staring her daughter down. There had been a few boys on base that Julianna got caught making out with and had been grounded shortly. Julianna shuddered at the thought of being that way with Roman. Ick he was practically an old man.

"Gross, Mom, now I won't be able to eat dinner."

"For one night I am asking you to be polite and try to show a genuine interest in him. Make some small talk with him. Boys like to feel needed and you can show him it's okay to have fun and not be serious all the time. Hey, maybe we can play some board games after dinner!"

The groan wail that came out of Julianna was pure teenager. She was taking time to focus on herself and not worry about dating or flirting, although she wouldn't mind having a significant other, it just was too messy. This was her fresh start in a new place and she wanted to scope out everyone before making any moves on anyone.

The car ride was much quieter than the one home from school. It also felt way too short. Julianna was all smiles and politeness, even though she was seething on the inside. Val and Esteban were great, she didn't know how their son was so dull. She told herself it wouldn't be all bad and Val was a great cook. Everyone hugged and said their salutations on the way to the kitchen. The table was set with wine for the adults and a pitcher of sweet tea for the kids. Val had gone all out with homemade tortillas, vegetables fresh from the garden, and slow cooked ropa vieja. There were beans, rice, and something on the counter that Julianna hoped was sliced plantains. Those had always been her favorite when coming over for dinner when she was younger.

Her mom and Valerie had set it up so she had to sit next to Roman. He smiled nicely at her and passed her everything so she could serve herself first. They held hands and said a small blessing before they all began to eat. The mothers dominated the conversation thankfully. Every time they spoke they tried to pull Julianna and Roman into talking, but they both kept their words short and brief. When everyone was finished they cleared the table and loaded the dishwasher while Valerie fried up plantains for dessert. They ate them with some vanilla ice cream and there were no leftovers. Esteban excused himself to go watch TV and Valerie and Angelica went to their spot on the back porch to talk. This left Julianna alone with Roman. They were so wildly different, but her mom's speech earlier made her feel sad for Roman. Little did she know that Val had given him much the same speech, except about her.

"So that was a pretty great first day. I bet you're anxious to graduate, though. You've had plenty of first days now." she smiled weakly while trying to start a conversation.

"Eh, I guess. Basketball practice starts next week. I'm just trying to stay on top of my classes so I can play without stressing on any assignments. I don't procrastinate because I can't play if I'm worried about finishing anything." Roman was examining his fingernails while talking.

"Oh. Well, maybe we can come to a few of your games. I think my mom mentioned that. It'd be interesting to know someone on the court. Spectating has always been dull to me, but knowing the best player might make it better."

"For sure, I'd like that. I wouldn't want you to go if it wasn't your thing, though. Will you have any drum performances? I bet our moms will expect us to all go."

"Yeah, we should, and there will be a few events the band plays for the community. Maybe we can come and provide live music for basketball and volleyball, give the marching band a break."

Roman smiled, though he was screaming on the inside. That would be horrible. No one wanted to hear music from garbage cans at a sporting event. The marching band was bad enough trying to get everyone hyped up. To Roman it was all a bunch of noise and he would wear earplugs if he could to tune it out.

"Well, I do have some homework to do. I'll see you Wednesday in drama, have a good second day tomorrow."

Julianna watched Roman disappear into the house and sat alone in the kitchen. He didn't seem shy or like he had a crush on her. He just seemed boring. It was hard to keep conversations pleasant. She tried to joke and he took it seriously about having the steel drum band play for sport games. While he was so boring he didn't seem sad or depressed like her mom seemed to think. Just another awkward weirdo trying to fit into society's mold. She had been happily surprised to see him be able to do a simple improv assignment, and also surprised he knew what a motorcycle was. Roman? On a motorcycle? That would be hilarious to see, as far as she knew, he was still reluctant to learn how to drive.

She went into the living room and sat on the couch and watched some preseason football that Esteban had turned on. It seemed so counterproductive. Julianna was lost deep in thought when Angelica and Valerie came back inside laughing. Then they both noticed that Julianna was on the couch and Roman was gone.

"You doing okay? Where did Roman go?" Valerie said quietly.

"He said something about homework. I'm just watching some TV with Esteban, no big deal, I'm all good."

Both Valerie and Angelica shared a frown. Valerie started down the hallway when her husband called to her.

"Stop it. Give him some space and leave it alone right now. Don't meddle."

"Meddle? Meddle?! Is it meddling to make sure our son is being a gentleman? Is it meddling to expect him to be a gracious host?! It doesn't bother you that he won't entertain a friend for an evening? He abandoned her and holed himself in that room again!"

"He isn't a host to anyone, you invited your friend over and your friend has a daughter. He didn't invite anyone over. Besides, Julianna and I have been having a great time watching some football. I think she should join my fantasy league." Esteban winked at Julianna who beamed and giggled. Thank god he had some common sense.

"I'm fine Val. Really! I can amuse myself and don't need a playmate. I'd hate to distract him from his precious homework." Julianna batted her eyelashes with the last part and saw Roman appear behind his mom in the hallway.

"You guys alright? Everything okay?" Roman looked very confused.

"Well, I will see you tomorrow for lunch. It was great to get together with you Val, let's go J." Angelica gave Val a hug and Julianna waved goodnight to everyone.

Val shoved Roman in the shoulder and gave him a disapproving look as she walked them to the door.

"What'd I do?!" Roman looked around shocked.

"Nothing, son, don't worry. Go back to work." Esteban had already gotten involved in the game again. Roman stared bewildered at his mom, closing the door and turning around to glare at him. She shook her head and went back into the kitchen so Roman went back to his room thoroughly confused.

9 Romeo

He would never, in a million years, ever, admit that drama class was nowhere near as miserable as he thought it would be. A few weeks had passed and school had turned into a comfortable pattern again. Classes, homework, practice, studying, and soon games would be added in. The school had a block schedule so he enjoyed having fourth period being like an interactive brain teaser. It challenged him mentally and physically in a way that he never had to rise to. Memorization, thinking on his feet, being able to make his body move convincingly to play a role. His mother had been completely right, and he resented her immensely. But, don't forget, he would never let anyone know that.

Right now he was researching a monologue for the play tryouts. Mr. Henderson was still being extra secretive on what the play would be based on. The entire class was making up wild and crazy rumors about what would be coming up next. Last year it had been an adapted version of the <u>Pirates of Penzance</u> and the years before that featured <u>The Mouse Who Roared</u> and <u>Guys and Dolls</u>. A bunch of girls were hoping for <u>Westside Story</u> or <u>Romeo and Juliet</u>, but Roman was open to whatever was presented. He was having fun, but didn't want to take a real acting part from a kid who was truly interested and had looked forward to this class.

An accident. A completely random happenstance. There were worse things than winding up in this class, and it might just give him some good stories to tell through college. Spending his last year in high school taking a drama class was fitting, no one ever really knew what he was like and he felt like he was just acting out life sometimes. The few friends he had were close and knew him, but that was it.

The only problem was that Julianna had a crush on him, but Sloane had a crush on Julianna. Roman only knew these things because his mom and Mercutio told him about it. Roman didn't pick up on things like crushes or flirting or some subtle things and he didn't really care to. He was always the last to know about covert happenings and had to have people break things down very blatantly. Knowing a girl so much younger and different than him had a crush on him really weirded him out. Knowing his best friend's brother also was interested in her made him feel guilty for just existing. Sloane was great, and just a year older than Julianna, plus they seemed to have a lot more in common than he would with her. All of this meant he tried to be pleasant and friendly while simultaneously trying desperately to avoid her. This was almost impossible because Sloane always wanted to work with him, but Rose was comfortable working with both Roman and Sloane. So if Rose sat by them, Julianna would, too. Thank god Mr. Henderson kept mixing it up by having them get into randomized groups or whole class assignments. Today they had been assigned to find a monologue to memorize to help determine who would get what parts in the big performance.

There were piles of papers and books organized by gender, ages, comedy versus tragedy, classic, modern, and a stack of laptops for database searches. Groups were free to look through them and practice them as they wanted. Roman wedged himself into a theater seat and put his feet up on the back of the seat in front of him with his own laptop out. He had no clue what to look for. He'd find something and know it when he saw it. Other students had been through this before and had their own monologues picked out. The last few weeks they had had monologues assigned to them to practice in preparation for the big one. With actual basketball games starting Roman was more concerned with sports than finding a piece for drama class. He was focused now so he didn't have to worry about it later. He could practice in the car or at home, but he would have a solid choice before walking out today.

Tabs open, eyes scanning, he read through dozens of different monologues. From famous to obscure none were seeming just right. He looked around at the pairs and groups already practicing lines on each other. He saw Sloane, Rose, and Julianna laughing while passing stacks of papers back and forth to each other. While he didn't think himself quite antisocial, or even completely introverted, he felt this was a personal and private assignment. Roman didn't want to brainstorm, he just wanted to pick a good monologue, get a good grade, and get assigned to being a stagehand. He just needed something that fit.

Suddenly, he was on a page for a small community theater out in a town close to theirs. They had done different takes on famous poems and there were plays based around their lives and experiences. One was for an older teen and was interspersed with Lewis Carroll's <u>Jabberwocky</u>. Roman's dad had read him <u>Alice in Wonderland</u> and <u>Alice Through the Looking Glass</u> as a kid and he regularly reread them. It was fascinating how it could be a children's book, but also look at the society of the time. Word play, puzzles, logic, and puns all disguised as nonsense was the kind of thing Roman enjoyed thoroughly. No one that didn't know him personally would ever think he'd be so fond of something so seemingly frivolous.

He pulled out his phone to time himself reading it as Sloane suddenly was next to him.

"Hey man, what'd you find so far? Any luck?" Sloane plopped down next to him, startling him out of his focus.

"Oh, uh, yeah. I think so. Was just about to time myself reading it to make sure it isn't over five minutes." Roman pulled up a new tab just opened to the main search bar so Sloane couldn't see his page, "How about you? Did you find something?"

"Nah, all those papers are old. We mostly laughed at how cringey they are. Plus I did so many monologue lessons last year I'm a little tired of it. I might just redo an old one if Henderson is cool with that. He is pretty forgetful over time."

Roman nodded and smiled at Sloane. Sloane wasn't getting the hint that this wasn't something he wanted an audience for, yet.

"How about Rose and Julianna? Did they get settled?" Roman hoped bringing up the girls would get Sloane to leave.

"Kind of? They grabbed a couple of books to take home and look through and started talking about Tyler and their family and Julianna's dad should be home this month. I didn't really want to just be eavesdropping on them."

Roman's heart went out to Sloane. He was such a polite kid and didn't want to make anyone feel left out, but it seemed to happen to him all of the time. Roman could time himself later, he adjusted in his seat so Sloane couldn't see the screen while he copied the monologue, website he found it at, and a short email to Mr. Henderson making sure he got approval before reading it.

"It will be good for J's dad to be back in town. I've always felt bad for Rose having such a jerk of a brother. It sucks he didn't move out or leave town for college after graduating. He's still in town just lurking like a cockroach." Roman typed while he spoke.

"At least he isn't at school anymore and we can just avoid where he goes. Rose doesn't have that option. How can two kids from the same family turn out so differently?" Sloane looked across at Julianna and Rose laughing and reading.

"Tyler makes me glad I'm an only child, but you and Mercutio are the best siblings. I wish I had a brother sometimes, but it's still awesome to see both of you so much." Roman smiled at Sloane as he sent his email and packed up his laptop.

"Aw, thanks Roman. Mercutio and I fight sometimes, but yeah, I am so glad I have him instead of a Tyler. Ugh, I hate this assignment. I wish we just knew what the play was so we could take parts from it but NOOOOO Henderson decided it has to be a mystery."

"It'll be alright. You have two more years of drama to take if you want to keep trying. I'm looking forward to this being out of the way so I can focus on college next year."

"Oh I'll definitely keep taking drama! A few of my other senior friends get to go off campus to work at the community theaters. That volunteer work is giving them all kinds of experience and connections."

The bell rang, interrupting Sloane, and everyone left their separate ways.

10 Juliet

Julianna: MY DAD JUST GOT HOME!!!

Rose: WHAT??? AHH I'M COMING OVER!

Julianna: Not yet! Don't tell your mom! He wants to surprise her.

Rose: No fair!

Julianna: We're going to plan a get together, I've got to go. Dinner and family movie ^_^

Rose: <3

Juliana turned her computer off and ran back down stairs. Her dad had moved his bags into the bedroom and her mom was serving dinner onto the TV trays in the living room. Julianna got started on some air popped popcorn. Her mom didn't even know he was going to be home that day, so she couldn't cook him his favorite, but he was so glad to just be with his girls. After dinner they sat together on the couch, Julianna's dad in the middle with his arms around his wife and daughter.

They invited Rose's family over the next day, Sunday, for a barbeque. While it was nice to see Rose, Aunt Aly, and Uncle Will, Tyler was there, too. The girls stuck together and Tyler was a little bit more reserved around his dad and uncle. Everyone was thrilled that Charles was home and retiring from active duty. The guys grilled pork and drank some beers while the ladies set up some side dishes at the table outside. Charles loved to cook with his wife and together they made the best authentic Vietnamese dishes. There were fresh spring rolls in rice paper, bún thịt nướng for the main course, and fresh fruits and veggies on the side.

When everything was ready they sat on the porch and said grace before digging in. It had been close to five years since the last time all of them had sat and shared a family meal. Fall was setting in fast and soon it would be the winter holiday season.

"What about you Rose? How is your senior year going? You're going to be out of school just like your brother, that must be exciting!" Charles smiled at his niece warmly.

"Oh. I guess it's bittersweet. I really do like school and am having fun in drama. I'll also be doing a little bit of writing and taking pictures for the school newspaper at the basketball games coming up." Rose explained. She didn't like being the center of attention, but she was always happy to spend time with her uncle.

"Basketball sucks and nobody even reads the stupid school paper. I can't believe you are taking a full course load your last year when you could be taking it easy." Tyler blurted out coarsely.

"Oh is it? So why was it that you had to take a full course load and summer school every year?" William, Tyler's father, shot back, "Your sister is going to work hard and actually achieve something while you won't even take a few courses at the community college."

"Whatever. I'm so glad I'm out of high school. Not all successful people go to college, it's just a way to get programmed. I'm going to be a self made man." Tyler carried his plate into the kitchen and turned on the TV in the living room to sulk.

"Don't mind him, he's been working back to back shifts and trying to do better volunteering at that youth program." Aly filled in for her son.

Tyler had always been catered to by his parents and resented anyone besting him at anything. Rose was planning to move out at the end of the school year with a few close friends and share rent on an apartment. Working hard and avoiding attention came as naturally to her as slacking off and being a braggart came to her brother.

"Well I guess we will see you at the basketball game, Rose, we promised to go see Roman play this week!" Angelica smiled as she started clearing the table with everyone else.

"Roman! Now that is exciting, I heard he has made a name for himself on the court. I haven't seen him since he was just a little guy. Have you stayed close with him?" Charles smiled as he got utensils from around the grill to take back inside the house.

"Oh, uh, yeah we see each other. We went to prom last year, but that was just as friends. It's not like we go out of our way to see each other, though."

"Julianna told me he is in your drama class with Sloane. Both of you are fortunate to have such reliable boys as friends." Angelica touched Charles on the arm while she spoke and smiled at Julianna.

"Ugh, mom, you're making this weird."

"What? I didn't say anything weird! You think a girl would be lucky to have Roman as a boyfriend, right?"

Rose looked bewildered and saw Julianna fake gagging and Angelica glaring at her daughter.

"Mom thinks Roman is secretly in love with me and is mad that I don't "Make more of an effort" to woo him." Julianna finally said.

"Julianna!" Angelica rebuked her.

Everyone else was stunned, but Rose started laughing hysterically so hard that she had to sit down.

"Roman is queer!" Tyler shouted from the living room.

"No one asked you, ass, and even if he was that's not a bad thing!" Julianna shouted back.

"If you don't looooove him, why are you defending him? I should have kicked his ass for asking Rose out last year."

"Knock it off!" William stormed into the living room and roughly grabbed Tyler by the arm before Julianna could shout back at him again. They both went out the front door and it slammed behind them.

Everyone in the house uncomfortably started getting out ice cream sandwiches for dessert and sitting in the living room where they could hear muffled arguing from outside.

"I don't think Roman really likes anyone, not like that. He likes studying and competition, but he really doesn't give dating or romance a thought. If he liked someone he would tell them. I actually asked him out last year, because Mercutio asked me to." Rose ate her sandwich nervously.

William and Tyler came back in.

"Apologize to your family. Apologize to your sister and your cousin. You will not speak that way just because you have an inferiority complex!" William stood behind his son, hand on his shoulder.

"I'm sorry Rose. I'm sorry Julianna. If you want to hang out with dweebs, that is your problem." Tyler rolled his eyes as he gave the least sincere apology possible.

It wasn't long after that they all went home. Everyone had a busy new week ahead of them.

The week went by quickly and it was soon Friday. Julianna hung around campus that afternoon with Rose and Bethany until it was time for the game. They watched the team practice and the other school arrive for competition. Charles and Angelica came to the game together and sat with Roman's parents up in the bleachers. Rose stayed close to the action with her camera. Mercutio was keeping her company while she worked and Sloane was sitting off to the side messing around on his phone. Seeing that, Julianna told Bethany to grab some seats in front of her parents and dashed down to talk to Sloane.

"Sloane! Hey, what's up? Want to come sit up with us?" Julianna grinned and beamed positivity as she asked him.

Startled, Sloane had to take a moment to compose himself. This was the first time Julianna had initiated conversation with him outside of a classroom and without other friends close by. After what seemed an eternity he smiled and nodded. He followed Julianna up the bleachers like a puppy and said hello to the parents.

The game started and everyone was cheering and really into the game. Right when the first quarter was up Julianna looked across the gym. On the visitor's side she could see Tyler with some strange girl sitting on his lap. A couple of his friends were also there and they were laughing and making fun of the game. She could see Mercutio and Rose notice him and he started flipping them off while his friends shouted things she couldn't make out. Mercutio and Rose looked really upset and Julianna nudged her mom who had already been watching. Charles got up and made his way around the court. The second quarter had started in the meantime.

Every time Roman made a basket Julianna stomped the bleachers hard and cheered loudly for him. Soon she had Sloane and Bethany joining her. Their school's team felt unstoppable, a living organism totally in sync with controlling the game. Charles came back and Julianna saw Tyler and his friends loudly skulking out the back door. Julianna felt her dad squeeze her shoulder as he sat back down. Rose was looking towards them and gave a little thumbs up. The game was exciting and Julianna was surprised that she felt proud and happy for her school's team. Sports weren't something she really understood, but she could appreciate why other people liked them.

At the end everyone went down to talk to the team. Rose and Mercutio found Julianna and everyone.

"Great job, man!" Mercutio slapped Roman on the shoulder, "You want to go get some pizza?"

"Yeah that sounds good, I have to go into the locker room first. Meet you out back?" Roman was still breathing hard, but didn't seem tired.

"You should come, too, J! If that's alright with you guys." Rose smiled at Julianna's parents.

The adults all told their kids to not be home too late and said good-bye. Roman headed off to the locker room to get cleaned up and changed. The kids went out the back door toward the student parking lot. Mercutio got into his car to drive Sloane and Roman, but when he turned the key to start his car nothing happened. It was like his battery was dead. Rose had been ready to drive Julianna and Bethany so she pulled around in front to give him a jump. The battery wasn't dead. The battery cables had been cut.

The six teenagers stood around in disbelief. Mercutio sent a quick text to his parents letting them know what had happened. They told him to let the school know the car would be there until Monday and they would deal with it then. After talking with campus security they all got into Rose's van.

"That's the good thing about having a mom-car, I can help people out when they need it!" Rose said, trying to lift Mercutio's spirits. It didn't work and he kept fuming in the back seat.

Everyone was hungry when they got to the pizza place, which had an all you could eat buffet deal if the team won the Friday night game. The car delay had actually caused the restaurant to clear out as other groups had finished so there was plenty of pizza and space for them. Sloane sat next to Julianna again and she didn't move her knee away from his when he bumped into her. They were closing up the pizza shop and a guy came over to their table.

"Hey Mercutio, friends," the boy smiled at everyone, "You guys should go to the house party tonight! Chill out with some people, get to cut loose a little bit?"

"Sylvester! Guys, this is my good friend Sylvester. He is an absolute doll." Mercutio gushed as he spoke and excused himself to go talk with his friend.

"He graduated last year," Roman explained to everyone else. Sloane and Rose nodded, both being familiar with him previously.

"Okay so there is a house party, lots of chill people, what do you guys think? I mean, I'll see if I can go with him if you all can't, since I am a ride mooch for the evening." Mercutio filled them in when he got back.

"I'll go if mom and dad are cool with us going," Sloane pulled out his phone to text for permission.

Roman did some mental calculations and decided being Mercutio's keeper for a night was a better choice than going home and restudying the same lessons from the week. He would just worry about his friend being out late until he got home anyway. He texted his mom and got permission.

"You ladies in?" Rose asked Bethany and Julianna, "If not, I don't mind taking you both home first. Absolutely no pressure."

"Let me ask. Bethany, can you stay at my house after if it's okay with my parents."

In a few moments all the teens had contacted home and received permission with full plans going forward with the evening. They paid their tab at the cash register, left a generous tip for Sylvester, and loaded themselves into Rose's van.

11 Romeo

Parties were not Roman's thing. He was reserved and solitary. However, he didn't mind going out with friends to be there as a voice of reason. He never drank, but he also didn't drive so he was a useless designated driver. Still, he wouldn't hesitate to hide some car keys, call for a Lyft, and pay for it if it meant his friends got home safely.

The house was a rental for some nerdy college kids. Their idea of partying included binge watching B movies, trying out recipes from the internet, playing board games, and coming up with new mixed drinks to theme after the latest memes. Bethany, Sloane, and Julianna found a table and began playing dominos. Julianna was sitting across from Sloane and hanging on his every word. Please keep her away from me, Roman prayed in his mind.

Rose had her own bottle of water and had followed Mercutio to the backyard where there was a fire pit and outdoor pool table. A few kids congratulated Roman and they made small talk while Mercutio helped himself to the keg. Sylvester showed up after some time and took away Mercutio's attention. Rose kept playing pool and Roman found an upside down five gallon bucket to sit on by the fire. A group on the porch were sharing a hookah and there was a karaoke machine inside. It was nicer to be people watching outside.

"Oh how *terrible*. Absolutely horrific!"

Roman immediately tensed up. Tyler had walked up behind Mercutio and Sylvester. Rose excused herself from the game and walked over to Roman as Roman stood up. They walked over in front of Sylvester and Mercutio as Tyler and a girl stood behind them.

"What the hell are you doing here, Tyler?!" Rose growled. She was extremely angry that her brother always turned up when she was finally away from him.

"My lovely sister! It turns out that my girlfriend Courtney's cousin rents a room here. We are simply visiting her family. Why on earth are you out of the house so late? A lady shouldn't be out so late unescorted." He hugged the girl that was with him closer to his side.

"I am escorting my friends by being designated driver and not making people uncomfortable. Nobody wants you here." As Rose spoke the girl next to Tyler gave her a confused and unfriendly look.

"Rosesh ish fruckin' mazin' dude. Mazin'. Jus' be nice a her." Mercutio shook his finger back towards Tyler while speaking.

"Aw Mercutio, I heard you explaining to your buddy here about your bad car luck. That's really, really awful. I couldn't believe what I was hearing. I have a friend that works on cars, I'll text you his information." He leaned over and took Mercutio's phone to get his contact information, then he sent the shop address and name to him.

"Why are you being so nice tonight?" Roman asked, suspicious of him.

"I'm always nice. It's not my fault everyone is so damn sensitive to take a joke. Here, I'll go get everyone a drink while you guys keep Courtney company. She has been talking about how close she wants to be with you, Rose, isn't that right?"

"Huh? Oh, yeah, of course. See you soon, babe." Courtney gave Tyler a peck on the cheek and smacked his butt as he walked away.

Rose invited Courtney to play a round of pool with her. Roman joined them to get a feel of how genuine this girl was. Through talking they learned she was new to town and was going to college. She seemed fine and maybe Tyler was making some positive changes. No one could be a miserable cretin for their entire life, right?

Tyler came back with four drinks, a weird cocktail for Mercutio, a beer for Courtney, and some soda for Roman and Rose.

"I know you don't drink, Roman. Gotta keep that mind and body sharp for sports and school. Nothing to sully it. Go on, now, drink up. I really do feel bad for what happened to your friend tonight and how I always treat you like crap. Starting right now I am going to do anything I can to help you out, man. Seriously."

Roman looked at the cup and swirled it, looked through the bottom and side, and smelled it. He glanced at Rose and raised an eyebrow. She shrugged and took a drink. He finally took a few sips.

"Thanks Tyler. I hope you mean it. Let me know if you guys need anything."

"Of course! Enjoy your evening, see you all later."

Rose and Roman joined Mercutio and Sylvester as Tyler walked away with Courtney.

"That was very suspicious and unusual," Roman still was uncertain if he should drink the soda.

"You're telling me! Especially after the way they were acting at the game. I guess my uncle being home means he doesn't want any problems with our dad."

Rose filled them in on the awkward family barbeque.

"Yeesh. Tyler is a frucking ashloe. Hahaha." Mercutio put his arm around Sylvester and leaned his head on his shoulder as he laughed.

"Oh, man, I should go check on Sloane and the girls. You have a hold on Mercutio, guys?" Roman asked as he realized they had left a sophomore and two high school freshmen unattended at a college party. Who knew what kind of chaos Julianna could be wreaking on the inside. Rose and Sylvester shooed him away as he backed up inside.

The scene inside was not as crazy as he had been imagining. A group of kids were playing karaoke on the patio from the open door, a few others were playing Smash Brothers and taking turns, and he found Julianna with her friends playing Scrabble.

"Hey, how is it going in here? You guys having a good time?" Roman sat down at an empty seat.

"Great! We should start game night at our house after basketball games, what do you think? I'm going to ask Mercutio." Sloane was talking a mile a minute and grinning like a fool. Bethany and Julianna agreed and started telling Roman stories about how they went from playing dominos, to taking turns at karaoke, to getting Scrabble out. They had just ended a game and decided to play a new game with Roman. He was pleasantly surprised at how easy going Julianna seemed and wasn't getting any sort of love sick puppy vibe from her. Bethany on the other hand kept taking any opportunity to bump elbows or knees with him. It was annoying, but not all together so bad. She seemed like a really sweet girl. Everything was going great until Julianna suddenly stopped and stood up. She bumped the table and rattled all of the pieces all over.

"Who the fuck is that?" Julianna hissed as she pointed behind everyone else. The group turned to see a strange guy practically dragging Rose towards the hallway and back of the house. Before anyone else could react Julianna grabbed something out of her backpack, launched herself across the room, and grabbed the guy by the back of the shirt.

Before he even realized he had moved, Roman had awkwardly followed Julianna. Everything was moving like molasses and warp speed at the same time. He caught up just in time to catch a groggy Rose as the guy lost his grip. Rose was a slim, Amazonian goddess, but she was just a few inches shorter than Roman and it took some balancing to keep her steady. He felt pain in his wrist and winced.

"Whus up honey, you wanna get some, too? This tall one's into me. We're gunna go have some fun so if you aren't in getta hell outta here!" The sleazy rando reached out to grab Julianna.

That's all it took and he was suddenly on the floor screaming and clawing at his face.

"THIS ASSHOLE IS TRYING TO RAPE MY COUSIN! WHO THE FUCK IS THIS GUY?!" Julianna screamed and started kicking the guy in the side with her steel toed boots. He half crawled and half rolled away. He made it to his feet and to the door and ran off into the street. About ten people jumped up and chased after him.

A few more helped get Rose over to a couch and everything stopped. Rose was barely conscious and Sylvester came in with Mercutio. They got Rose her water and got her to drink a few sips. She was fairly incoherent and mumbling.

"We need to get her to the hospital." Roman said this firmly and calmly. Mercutio was starting to freak out and trying to find someone to fight. Bethany and Sloane were suddenly on the job of calming him down.

"I agree, but I don't want her to get in trouble with her mom or dad. They will absolutely flip out. If I call my mom they'll find out and if we call your mom my mom will find out." Julianna was digging her nails into her arms and shaking while trying to calm herself down. She walked over to Mercutio and Sloane. Bethany had tears running down her face. Party goers were arranging rides home.

"Sloane. Could we call your mom or dad? Could they help us out?"

"Y...yeah! We could do that. Mercutio. You gotta get it together. I'm calling mom and dad."

"Don't worry about him. I'll have him presentable and talk to my friends. I am so, so sorry guys. This has never happened before. This is a safe place." Sylvester was beside himself as he spoke.

Sloane called home while Julianna talked to the college kids that lived in the house. She explained that they had to call the police and make a report, but didn't want to get in trouble any more than they did. She said Bethany, Sloane, and herself hadn't drank and they'd let the police know that no underaged drinking had gone on and they'd all take breathalyzers. The plan was to leave Mercutio at home.

Mercutio and Sloane's parents met them at the house. Their dad took Mercutio home in their car and Sloane's mom took the rest to the emergency room. No one wanted to go home, they all wanted to stay and be supportive of Rose. She went back and received a bed while Julianna stayed right by her side. The doctors said she was fine, and hadn't had very much. They needed to know if she took any other medications recently or if she had been drinking. Date rape drugs can interact with medications people are on and cause death unintentionally. Julianna answered any and all questions since Rose was able to walk around with help, but wasn't ready to answer any questions. The doctors took a blood sample and urine sample to test for whatever she was given. Sloane and Mercutio's mom stayed with the girls the entire time. Everyone else was in the waiting room. Julianna came out and gave everyone a brief update, but went right back in.

"We have to do a police report," Mom said to Julianna. Everyone called her Mom. She was the de facto mom. Even to other moms she would mom at them. It was never condescending or hateful, it was just love. She was common sense and rationality personified.

"Will they tell her parents?" Julianna glanced nervously at Rose. Her parents were so strict and so hard. They would blame her for this, she wouldn't be a victim in their eyes.

"No, not if she doesn't want them to. She is the legal age of consent and the hospital keeps these things private. This was an assault and a violation, it could have been a lot worse if you hadn't been there. You are a guardian angel of vengeance and fury. I am proud of you and so glad you were there to protect her. I'm also so glad my sons have made such good, dependable friends."

The police came in. They took information from everyone. Location, time, and gave all the kids breathalyzers. Everything checked out. Rose was very shaky and didn't remember much of the night. No one knew the guy, but they gave a good description. The police left to follow up with the kids at the party and reassured Rose and Julianna that they would keep everything confidential. There was little hope that they would find out who did it, but it was always good to have a report on file just in case anything came to light.

The hospital discharged Rose and Mom drove everyone home. She dropped Bethany and Roman off first, then Rose and Julianna at Julianna's house. They got in and upstairs quietly. Julianna peeked into her parents room and let them know she was home and Rose was staying over. They texted Rose's parents to give them a heads up as well. Mom said that in the morning Mercutio would pick Rose up and bring her back to her van. Everyone was safe and exhausted. Parties wouldn't be enticing for anyone anytime soon.

12 Juliet

Monday. Last Monday she had been glowing that her dad had come home finally and was looking forward to a basketball game. Today she was still coming to terms with what had happened Friday. Rose had filled her in on what had happened after she went home. Tyler hadn't gone home Friday night or Saturday night. He came home in the afternoon Sunday and stayed in his room. Their parents had no idea what had happened. Hers didn't either, for that matter.

Julianna desperately wanted to tell her mom and her dad, but if she told them everything, they in turn would tell Rose's parents and her parents were not the parents that could make rational decisions.

In the midst of all the turmoil she forgot to practice her monologue for class. It was tryout week and she was not prepared. For once she got to class early and went up to Mr. Henderson and asked if it would be okay if she went Friday. He made a quick note and let her know not to stress out about it too much. She hated not going first, truth be told. It was way better for her to get performances or auditions out of the way. Watching everyone else go made it agonizing when it finally was your turn and it was so much more pressure.

She picked her spot and shoved her backpack in the seat next to her for Rose and Bethany when she heard the door open and Sloane and Roman walked in. She looked at Roman and her heart ached. His left arm was wrapped in a splint and some athletic tape. When he caught Rose his wrist was sprained from grabbing her awkwardly and making sure she didn't fall over. Julianna fretted over how that would affect his basketball games this season. Mr. Henderson got up and talked to the boys, but she couldn't make out what they were saying. She had her monologue out and had started working on it, but now it was too distracting. The boys came down to sit behind her, which was a change, because they normally sat in the back by themselves. She turned around in the seat and sat backwards to talk with them.

"Hey Sloane, hey Roman. You guys have a better weekend after Friday night?"

"Hi J, yeah, everything quieted down. Are you holding up alright, have you talked with Rose?" Roman smiled as he talked.

"We're fine. She's shooken up, but mostly because she doesn't remember anything herself and that's frustrating. Everyone telling her stuff in bits and pieces. I'm sorry about your arm, is it very bad?" Julianna nodded towards Roman's sling.

"Oh, yeah, it's worse because I didn't get it taken care of right away. I told my parents I must have jammed it from stumbling at the party. I'll be fine in a week or so, nothing broken. I feel like a wuss getting an injury from just catching a girl. Were you practicing your monologue?"

Julianna glanced down at her paper and back up at the boys. She smiled as she answered, "Yeah, I totally spaced it after Friday night. I talked to Mr. Henderson about going later in the week. What about you guys?"

"Oh, well, I am monologuing for a play from last year so I'll go today just to get it out of the way." Sloane said nonchalantly.

"I'm going to go today, too. Better to get the grade in the grade book and focus on making some backgrounds and getting set to be a stagehand." Roman started to pretend to crack his knuckles as he spoke, but realized they were taped up.

"You're both nuts. But if you're ready you're ready. Are you really okay, Roman? I'm glad you were there to help, but I feel awful that this will screw up basketball."

Roman nervously touched his wrist as he answered carefully, "It's fine, really. I have to sit out of practice and the game this week, but next week they should be fine. It's nothing that will be a big deal, there are plenty of guys on the team that will keep us from being slowed down."

He winked at Julianna. She panicked. Flirting?! Was he actually flirting with her? Was her crazy mother right? No, that was a blink, a weird one eyed blink-wink. Before she could spiral any further the bell had rang and Rose and Bethany came in. They sat on either side of her and she put her head on Rose's shoulder and reached around to squeeze the other side.

"Alright everyone! Monologue time! We have seventy minutes to go through and hear some great monologues. We will be recording them so the team of producers can review which people would be best for the various roles. Don't be nervous, relax, and have fun!"

With that the auditions started. Sloane went up and did a short comedic monologue that really loosened the class up. Everyone applauded as he came down and Julianna reached behind and gave him a high five and knuckles for a job well done. Four more students went up and did great. One girl said a line twice, but finished strong. Roman was called up to be the last for the day.

He stood on the stage and looked very strong for how banged up he was. He took a breath in and out, looked down for a moment, and then locked his gaze on the audience.

"You never know where you will find friends. The kind that make sure you're okay and the ones where it's relaxing to hang out without saying anything at all. Those kinds of friendships are rare and valuable."

Roman gave a small, barely noticeable nod towards Sloane and Rose. His voice was calm, cool, and confident. The next part he boomed:

"'Twas brillig, and the slithy toves
Did gyre and gimble in the wabe:
All mimsy were the borogoves,
And the mome raths outgrabe."

What? What was that?! Nonsense poetry? He suddenly went back to his original voice.

"Interacting with strangers is draining. Trying to figure out their motives and their subtle nuances. I can't stand any of that. It's much better to stay inside with a good book and to let the world handle itself."

That sounded like Roman. One hundred percent. That wasn't even a stretch Julianna thought.

"'Beware the Jabberwock, my son!
The jaws that bite, the claws that catch!
Beware the Jubjub bird, and shun
The frumious Bandersnatch!'"

Julianna sat up even taller. She knew this poem! It was familiar, but it didn't go with the other stuff he was going on about.

"Our parents warn us and try to teach us as much as they can to keep us safe. We obey and listen as best as we can. Always looking out for the next Jabberwock, Jubjub bird, or even a Bandersnatch. These threats come to us, can harm us, even if we do everything right in

the world. Follow all the directions and try our best to not make any waves."

This was fantastic. He was like two people in one on the stage. A poet and a narrator. A bard and a sage. Julianna looked around and the entire audience sat breathless as if they had been turned to stone by his very words.

"He took his vorpal sword in hand;
Long time the manxome foe he sought—-
So rested he by the Tumtum tree
And stood awhile in thought."

Julianna sat just as mesmerized as everyone else as Roman paced back and forth on the stage with an invisible sword in his hand. He found a table on stage and leaned on it.

"Society wants to keep us fighting all kinds of monsters and not to rest and think. Keep going, be afraid, look out, and take care of yourself. So many of these monsters are products of nothing more than our own imaginations. People so often get caught up in whatever is going on in their lives and assume everyone else should be on high alert."

He went from being relaxed and wistful to jumping back and pantomiming an attack. The class gasped at the sudden change.

"And, as in uffish thought he stood,
The Jabberwock, with eyes of flame,
Came whiffling through the tulgey wood,
And burbled as it came!"

Roman's look of fear and determination in a fight melted away. He kept pretending to fight, but switched back to the casual, narrator-speak.

"Myself? I keep myself at arms length. I don't want to get into anything that is going to be complicated or confrontational. I'm not

disloyal or afraid to make a stand, I'm not even a coward. I just refuse to be beholden by the human instinct of needing to always find controversy. If you are so preoccupied by looking out for danger the only thing accomplished is causing conflict."

Julianna blinked. She never realized what made Roman tick. Why he was so unusual in such a boring and bland way? If you're going to be unconventional, make it exciting. Wait, no, this isn't him. He is acting, he's not talking about how he really feels. This whole act was convoluted and confusing.

"One, two! One, two! And through and through
The vorpal blade went snicker-snack!
He left it dead, and with its head
He went galumphing back."

He dropped the imaginary sword. He turned and did a modified gallop across the stage. He smiled with a cocky confidence that was not off putting.

"With razor sharp focus you can conquer any obstacle. Just focus on the end goal and don't let childish emotion get in your way. Other people just don't get it, the superficialness of this world and how pointless it is to spend our time being angry. I wish there was a way to make anybody else understand. Half of people think you're heartless, and the other half think you're naive. Both hate you for it."

Julianna was completely blown away. This was a boy she knew her entire life, but did not know at all.

"And hast thou slain the Jabberwock?
Come to my arms, my beamish boy!
O frabjous day! Callooh! Callay!"
He chortled in his joy."

"I do wish that I had learned how to have fun. How to enjoy myself and not be constantly driven to be better. That's the only way

I am going to stay ahead of the game in this competitive world. Work hard. Be honest. And not lower myself down to anyone's petty level. That's why it's so hard to truly know who is your friend."

"'Twas brillig, and the slithy toves
Did gyre and gimble in the wabe:
All mimsy were the borogoves,
And the mome raths outgrabe."

"Maybe I'm the Jabberwock. The last outhold on Earth against this lunacy our species is hurtling towards. My peers and the ones around me feel like constant threats. Out to behead me for their own gain. Murderous ruin and contempt hides behind vapid grins. Each one of them wants me dead. And so I stay in and read. Knowing that it is safer than being out and risking a thing."

Roman stood still in the center of the stage. He wasn't quite sure what came next. Julianna stood up and started clapping. Next came Mr. Henderson along with Sloane, Bethany, and Rose. The entire class was cheering and standing and clapping. Roman looked completely surprised and a little scared. He gave a shaky bow and dashed down the stairs back to his seat. The bell rang and Mr. Henderson hollered out encouragement for a fabulous first day and for everyone to be ready for Wednesday.

13 Romeo

The next time the class met Roman got to class early as he always did. Somehow not only had Julianna beat him to class early, but Bethany, Rose, Sloane, and even Mercutio were hanging around. Mr. Henderson came out of his office with a cup of noodles and motioned for Roman to come in to talk to him. Roman nodded to his friends and went into the sound room.

"Roman! I just knew you would be a natural. I already shared the audition tape with the team and they think you are going to be a shoe in for the lead! What do you think?" Mr. Henderson grinned between rushed bites of noodles.

"L... uh excuse me, did you say lead?"

"I did."

"But the auditions aren't done and I wasn't trying for a role. I was just having fun. I'd be much happier being behind the scenes. Lighting, being a stagehand, nothing fancy!"

Mr. Henderson scoffed, "Psch you would be wasted with your talent, your presence! You really have no idea how wonderful you were?"

Roman racked his brain. The mass hysteria of Monday he had chalked up to Julianna being insane and riling up the class. This had to be her fault. He wasn't any better than anyone else. This was a misunderstanding.

"Look, Mr. Henderson, no offense. I did not take this class on purpose. It was an accident because my counselor screwed up my credits. I've got a lot of practices for basketball and volleyball and plenty of AP classes. I'm working towards academic and athletic scholarships and this was not part of the plan. I don't want to take away anything from another student who took this class on purpose. That's not right for them, that isn't fair."

The look of disappointment on Mr. Henderson's face was palpable. He looked as if Roman told him that he would rather kick puppies around than be in this class. An uncomfortable silence hung between the two.

"Roman, I've had this job for a long time and I understand how important setting yourself up for the future is. I also have seen students go on to acting schools and have the desire to be a performer, but not have the talent. You are a natural. You worked hard, memorized the lines, and I was blown away with your performance. By far you are the most talented student I've ever had and the first quarter is barely done."

Roman stared at Mr. Henderson. As far back as Roman could remember he wanted to be something important. Make an impact on the world that would lead to positive change. He was never sure what the specifics were, but he didn't want to set any unrealistic goals for himself. It was also super hard for him to be selfish.

His train of thought was interrupted by Mr. Henderson again, "I'll tell you what. I can't decide anything for certain until we finish auditions. Although, it wasn't solely your audition that is making me feel this way. You've excelled and grown from every lesson and assignment this quarter. After auditions finish I can let you know what the play is and what the role is. If you don't want to, I'll skip over you and this will be just between us. No harm, no foul. This is your last chance to try something like this before graduating. We can work rehearsal schedules around games and practice. I want to work with you and I want you to be successful here."

Roman nodded as the bell rang, he passed Mercutio as he was leaving and they shared a high five. He sat down with Sloane and everyone and they sat back for a round of new auditions.

Friday was the final day of auditions and Julianna finally got to go. She did much better than most, but forgot a few lines. Roman clapped for her, but didn't try to start a standing ovation. He was still worried that she had feelings for him, but didn't want to give her the wrong idea. His mom still brought up him going out with her regularly.

Class ended and he went to the basketball game. It was an away game so he had to change and get onto the bus with the team. Even though he was benched he needed to attend games to support everyone. This time the team lost, but it was fairly close. His parents were there and sat by Julianna's again. Rose and Mercutio weren't there for the away game and that was fine. The two families went out for dinner at an Italian restaurant with no incidents like the previous week. Their moms orchestrated it so they had to sit next to each other at dinner, but they didn't straight up try and push an arranged marriage this time.

His wrist was feeling better by the weekend, but he was going to keep the splint on until an appointment on Monday. Better safe than sorry with any sort of sports injury.

Finally it was a new Monday and finally Mr. Henderson was going to reveal what the big, top secret play was. It was so far into the year and kids were anxious to get all of the details and parts sorted out. Roman was more concerned about finding out if his wrist was game ready than play details. Mr. Henderson had two, young college students with him. The man and woman were wearing university polos and were so fresh and crisp it was as if they had walked out of a recruitment catalog.

"Hello everyone! Today is the day we discover what this year's big performance will be! I'd like to start by introducing Candice and Brendan. They are going to be student observers as we work together on performing a never before seen show."

Mr. Henderson paused for the confused murmur that traveled through the class. New show? Never performed? The anxiety and curiosity was unbearable.

"I was blessed to be included in a seminar last summer through the university with the goal of preserving tales from the past while at the same time updating them for a modern audience. So many stories have been misrepresented from even older myths and are not always "politically correct". If we can go back to the base story instead of the censored and rewritten adaptations it can show how our ancestors are more the same than different from us."

The entire class was perplexed on different levels. Roman didn't care for censorship, but reclaiming lost stories sounded interesting.

"Candice and Brendan are both graduate students pursuing their masters that assisted in rewriting the 1926 Italian opera by Giacomo Puccini, Turandot!"

The excitement and joy at the reveal on Mr. Henderson's, Candice's, and Brendan's faces were perfect foils to the confused and clueless teenagers. They had been anticipating a well known and fun performance. No one had been prepared to be a guinea pig for some grad students' thesis. The class fidgeted uncertainly as Mr. Henderson continued. Candice and Brendan passed out copies of the script which included a preface detailing the history of the story.

"Giacomo Puccini based his opera off of a play by Carlo Gozzi written in 1762. Carlo Gozzi had been inspired by a 12th century Persian poet named Nizami. Nizami's epic poem, *Haft Peykar*, or

The Seven Beauties, was associated with the days of the week and the colors and planets that corresponded with them. In the original work the princess Turandot was known as Turan-Dokht and was to be a Russian princess. She told the story in the poem that inspired the play, that inspired the opera.

Through the years the story changed the princess from Russian to Chinese as translations and political borders evolved. Our goal was to transform the story closer to the original Persian roots and create something appropriate for high school students to perform. The original epic poem is a testament of the interconnectedness between various cultures and with each new iteration the story has evolved to show a changing and innovative style. Your homework is to not only read the script, but to write up a thousand word literary analysis of one of the versions discussed in the historical preface. When you understand the history you can gain a deeper appreciation for unfamiliar cultures."

The remainder of the class was spent watching some of the opera from 1926 performed by a contemporary theater company. Roman was called out of class shortly after the film started to have the appointment for his wrist.

The doctor removed the splint and said he could begin practicing and playing in games again, but to take it slowly. Sports had never been his sole option, but the fact that it could so easily be ruined by just an accident had really shaken him up. His mind was so full of everything from the party incident, to his studies, college, and the play. He hadn't looked at the characters yet, the story and the history sounded fascinating, but what was the story about? He would have to go home and read through the script. What should he tell Mr. Henderson? It was a huge decision and there were so many variables to weigh.

"Roman, we aren't going to go straight home. Angelica wanted me to go help her with some work at the gallery so we will be stopping there first," His mom broke his train of thought suddenly.

"Oh. Uh, well, since it is close to the mall would it be alright if I went there first? I'd like to see if I could talk to Mercutio about some things, he was going to grab any assignments I wasn't able to get."

The mall was fairly empty for an afternoon. He had texted Mercutio to meet him by a fountain in the food court and sat down to wait for him. He was reading through the character descriptions after the preface and felt hands suddenly fall over his eyes.

"Guess who!" the voice teased in a sing song.

Oh no. No.

"J, what are you doing?" Roman flailed as she removed her hands laughing.

"Calm down, nerd, you'll hurt your wrist again. It's good to see the bandage off, did the doctor give you the all clear?" Bethany and Rose were with Julianna and pulled up an extra table and chairs.

"Yeah, it's fine, I just have to take it slow. I'm just waiting for Mercutio to get here to tell me what I missed for the end of the day."

At that moment the four saw Mercutio and Sloane walking up to them. They all sat down and almost immediately started filling in Roman and Mercutio about the play.

"Ok, so the story focuses on a princess who doesn't want to get married. She has three riddles and to marry her you have to get all three of them correct. If you agree to the challenge and get any of them wrong you are executed! She lined the path to the palace with severed heads on spikes!" Bethany started explaining.

"That would be some fun prop making," mused Sloane.

"Think they'd notice if we made them look like different teachers?" Julianna grinned wickedly. She was thinking of Mr. DeSalvo and Mrs. Cummings.

"Wait, that's the play and opera that just focuses on the one princess. In the original poem it is about a king who goes around the world and marries seven different princesses. Each princess tells a different story and is from a different country that goes with a planet, color, and day of the week. The princess Turandot is red for Mars and Tuesday. So there are six other princesses that have a unique story, but the play and opera focused on the story of the red princess." Rose filled them all in.

"The god of war and red certainly makes sense, what with the beheadings. You must have really read the historical preface, Rose," Roman said.

"Yeah, I'm not big on having to read subtitles, so I only partially watched the opera. Mr. Henderson lent me a copy of the English translation of the epic poem, so I already started reading it. It'll be hard to limit my paper to only a thousand words! I want to write a synopsis comparing and contrasting each of the stories of the princesses. Maybe one of their stories is even more compelling to a modern audience than Turandot would be."

"Overachiever, like always!" Mercutio teased.

"I'm just trying to have some fun by getting immersed in the story! It isn't fun if I can't get involved in it. Besides, if those college students have to do stuff like this for their classes, it will be good practice for next year, right?" Rose tried to justify.

"That makes sense, but I'm not going to focus more on my drama class assignment than on my core classes. It's fun that the stories are interesting and kind of obscure, but I don't need any distractions," Roman fidgeted nervously while he spoke. No one knew what Mr. Henderson had said to him about getting the lead role. He still hadn't had time to process what all the different parts were.

"So instead of a king there is a prince and a princess, that's about all I got from what I've read and heard. How many parts are there?" Roman gestured to the open page of the cast of characters in front of him.

"So there are ten major roles and then some as commoners. There is the princess, her servants, her father, a king that has lost his kingdom, that king's servant, and a stranger who is actually the deposed king's son! Like so many other suitors he falls instantly in love with the princess and decides to take on the challenges," Bethany was taking on the explaining now. Roman flipped through his script until he got to the page with all of the characters listed. He read it while she kept talking:

<u>Nasrin-Nush: A Retelling of Turandot and The Seven Beauties</u>
<u>(Haft Peykar)</u>

Cast of Characters:

Princess Nasrin-Nush——————————-—A Slavic Princess Determined to Stay Unwed

King Mikhail ——————————————Father of Nasrin-Nush

Giacomo———————————————Servant of the Royal Family

Antonio——————————————-—Servant of the Royal Family

Puccinio—————————————— —Servant of the Royal Family

Executioner——— ——————————— ——Beheads Those Who Fail the Riddle Challenge

Watchman———————————————————Guards the Castle

King Harold——————————————————Deposed King of a Nordic Country in Exile

Prince Bjorn————————————————Son of King Harold

Kari——————————————————————Servant of King Harold

Common People—————————————-The Citizens of Princess Nasrin-Nush

"So with the amount of people in our class, it should be pretty easy to take a pass on an acting part and just work behind the scenes. With auditions done, what do you think the final cast list will be?" Roman tried to ask nonchalantly.

His friends stared emotionlessly at him, except Mercutio who was paying more attention to his phone game than the school conversation taking place around him.

"You aren't getting away with hiding behind the curtain, Roman," Rose said decisively.

"You should be the Prince, man, that audition was astounding!" Sloane was beaming.

"No, I mean, no. It was gibberish. Anyone could have done that. You just read the words, then say the words, it wasn't even hard. I don't want that kind of attention."

"Roman you really did do great, I don't think anyone would argue that you don't deserve that lead role. That would be a shame for our class, for the school, to not have you be in the starring role. I'll pitch a fit if you don't get it! I mean, if you really would prefer, you could be a stagehand and spend more time with me. I know my audition was rough, but that's okay. I'd rather play an instrument if there is any music in the play," J tugged on her sleeve while she spoke.

Roman sighed, put his head in his hands, looked back up at all of his friends and blurted out, "Mr. Henderson told me on Wednesday he wanted me in the lead role and with everything that is going on I am completely freaking out. How the hell has this even happened?!"

Everyone was stunned at his outburst, Roman was typically very soft spoken.

Everyone was stunned, except for Mercutio. With his eyes still on his phone he murmured, "Destiny."

"What?" Roman asked threateningly.

"It's destiny, man, stop questioning it and just go with it. You aren't supposed to fight fate this hard. It's going to happen, so let it happen. Your transcripts getting screwed up, only being able to take drama, this weird play all points to you not having enough excitement in your life and the more you resist the more strangeness you're going to get."

"I don't want excitement! I want to be left the hell alone!"

"Then just go with the flow and the universe will stop messing with you. You make yourself a target, you know that, right?" Mercutio had put down his phone and started to open a straw for his drink. He blew half of the paper at Roman who angrily batted it away.

"I hope you all realize you are putting me underneath unfair peer pressure and this is blatant bullying and harassment." Roman stared sullenly at his friends.

"But it's peer pressure of love!" Rose hopped out of her seat and hugged him from behind, and was soon joined by Mercutio,

Sloane, and J. Roman struggled, complained, and cursed until they finally let him go.

They left the mall together and on the drive home he stared at the script in his lap. He had one night to make up his mind on what to do so Mr. Henderson could assign roles. He stayed up most the night making pro/con lists and trying to create a schedule for the next three quarters.

14 Juliet

Julianna got home and started flipping through some homework. It was nice being at a "normal" school instead of being home schooled or going to a school on base. The workload was manageable, but the start of second quarter meant that the assignments were starting to pick up steam and could easily get out of hand. Steel drum had been a lot of fun so far and the class was pretty full so she could blend in, plus the teacher was laid back and didn't talk down to any of the students.

It was kind of strange being back in her childhood home. Things were more different here and in the town than they were the same. Same setting, same people, but time changed and warped everything. High school was a blast and it was a shame she had screwed up her audition for the play. Reflecting on it, she was just a freshman and she had never taken any drama or acting classes before. The night of the party was extremely stressful and both J and Rose were falling behind in their classes. There was also the matter of J using her pepper spray. She was only thirteen and not allowed to buy any, much less supposed to take it with her to school. Her mom had given it to her, for when she was out alone, but never expected her to actually use it. Now she had. If she asked her mom for more, her mom would have to be told why she used it. J decided she would talk to Rose, who was a few months away from turning eighteen.

She finished up her late assignments, emailed a few papers, took a shower, and was just climbing into bed when there was frantic knocking at the front door. Her upstairs window faced the side of the house, so she quickly made her way down the stairs as her father opened the door to a sobbing Rose bursting in. It had been raining and Rose was soaked, without a jacket, and only her backpack. J grabbed towels from the hall closet, Angelica had Rose sit down on the couch, and Charles went to make some coffee in the kitchen.

After a few minutes, Rose calmed down. She had a bruise forming on her cheek and sipped carefully from the coffee mug she had been given. Charles handed her a bag of frozen peas and she wrapped it in a towel and held it to her face.

"We had just finished dinner and I went to get my backpack. It wasn't hanging in the entryway, when I turned around, Tyler was holding it open and screaming at me. I had boxes of condoms to donate for my internship at the clinic, we had a drive at school and I was going to deliver them tomorrow. He started yelling at my dad and mom that I was a whore and was sleeping with the whole town. I tried to explain it was for my internship, but they didn't want to listen to me. I accused him of cutting Mercutio's battery cables and he hit me. When my dad went to yell at Tyler, he had pictures of the guy from the party with his hand down my shirt and making out with me. My dad kicked me out and told me he had no daughter and not to come back."

Once it was all out she started sobbing all over again. Angelica looked at Charles and J looked at both of her parents.

"You aren't going back there. You are staying here. I will get your stuff and you can stay home from school tomorrow. I won't let anyone, anyone, treat my niece this way, do you understand," Charles had gotten down on one knee next to Rose and held her unbruised side of her face in his hand.

She nodded shakily through her tears. Angelica had her phone out and a notepad which she wrote down the important details of what had happened. J hugged Rose and told her it was going to be okay.

"We are going to have to file a police report against Tyler. This will unfortunately, probably, just be chalked up to a domestic violence situation. It will help you get an order of protection and help us get some guardianship papers to tide us over until you turn eighteen. Now, what about a guy at the party? Is that anything I need to know about before I make this call?" Angelica looked over at the girls concerned.

"It's okay, J, you can tell her," Rose nodded and shut her eyes tight as she spoke.

"Well, remember after the basketball game we went for pizza and then went to Mercutio's friend's party?" Julianna began and looked at both of her parents who nodded, "Well, I stayed inside with Bethany and Sloane playing Scrabble. Roman, Mercutio, and Rose were outside playing pool. No one was drinking alcohol from our group except Mercutio. Tyler showed up with a girlfriend and Roman decided to come inside and play Scrabble with us. A little bit after that I saw Rose being dragged to the back of the house by some drunk guy. I confronted him, sprayed him with the mace you gave me, kicked him in the kidneys, and he ran out before anyone could catch him."

"You did *what*?!" Angelica said in a cool, icy voice.

"Let her finish, Ang, this has been taking a toll on both of them," Charles didn't sound much more pleased than his wife did as he spoke.

"S... So Tyler wasn't there anymore, and we didn't want the kids who lived at the house to get in trouble. They didn't know who the drunk guy was. We called Mercutio's mom and took Rose to the hospital. We made a police report, because, we were scared, we were scared of how Rose's dad would act if he," J couldn't keep explaining it anymore. It had been so terrifying. No one had gotten really hurt, but it made her feel vulnerable and scared for her cousin. For her friends. She never kept things from her parents and that had been the worst part of all. J was crying now, but felt relieved to not have the burden over her anymore.

Charles got more coffee, this time for everyone, and sat between his daughter and niece on the couch while they both cried all over again. Angelica called 911 and began the process of reporting the abuse. It was well after midnight by the time the officers arrived. A younger man with an older female officer. They had a print out of the prior report and the case of the guy who could have spiked Rose's drink. They questioned the parents first, then each of the girls separately.

"The case against the man who tried to take you into the bedroom. We have no eyewitness description that gives us enough details, and we aren't even sure if he is the one who spiked your drink. It sounds like, and I hate to say this, that your brother could have also been the culprit," The female officer glanced around the room and saw that while the adults didn't look shocked, the girls sure did.

"Tyler, did that to me on purpose?" Rose questioned.

"Well, we are reviewing the security video from the school to see who vandalized your friend's car. He has a history of aggression and petty crimes. From his actions and behaviors that's all we can surmise. Do you remember anything from the night at the party?" the male officer asked Rose gently.

"No. I barely remember the basketball game. I just have my notes and pictures. Roman was there! He was outside with me before he went inside. We weren't drinking because I drive and he is responsible."

The officers took down the information from the girls and said they would go to the school in the morning to get stories from Mercutio, Sloane, and Roman. They were headed over to Rose's house to talk to her parents and Tyler.

"Sometime this week you will have to come into the courthouse and file for guardianship and an order of protection from that side of the family. Do not go over there, do not call them, and if they show up here or at school call 911 immediately do not engage them." The officers left and the girls were left looking at Angelica and Charles.

"J, I understand why you didn't tell us, why you didn't call us. I'm hurt, but I'm not mad or disappointed. That was a hard thing and I am so sorry you had to go through that alone." Angelica gave Julianna a big hug.

"I'm so sorry mom. I'm so sorry. You're going to tell Valerie, aren't you? She is going to be mad at us. She's going to be so mad at Roman." Julianna was almost crying again.

"Oh honey! Are you worried about him? You do have feelings for him! I'll have lunch with her tomorrow, but if anything I think she'll be proud he finally did something borderline delinquent. Protecting girls and being responsible probably won't get him kicked out, though. I think she might be relieved that he kept a secret from her like a normal kid!" Angelica startled them by laughing.

"He is a normal kid, Ang, we should all try and get some sleep, okay?" Charles helped the girls get set up in Julianna's room. They would set the guest room up for Rose in the morning.

Julianna and Rose stayed home on Tuesday. They were happy that Charles hadn't found a job yet and was able to stay there and keep them company. Through texting with the boys they found out that Roman had only drank a little bit of his soda and went inside, leaving it outside. He never felt bad, except for his wrist. It could have been Tyler that roofied his drink and Rose accidentally drank it, or he roofied both, or the random guy had done it. It didn't matter, because without more evidence or a confession there wasn't enough to do anything about it legally.

This also meant that all three groups of parents were going to be talking. The kids were worried they wouldn't be allowed to see Sloane or Mercutio, but Angelica was grateful for their mom being able to handle the situation and get that initial police report started. Everyone was banned from going to parties for the rest of the year, however. Mercutio was the only one grounded, because he was drinking, but he was allowed to have friends over for supervised game nights, just like Sloane had wanted.

Angelica got some makeup and a few outfits for Rose while she was out. Underwear, socks, a pair of shoes, and some toiletries made her feel a little better. The police had let her family know that all of her important possessions would be transferred to Rose at a later date. Tyler had not been home when they got there to question him the night before. The court date was set for the Friday after Thanksgiving so Rose wouldn't have to miss school.

On Wednesday Rose was ready to go back to school and try to maintain a normal routine. Since her dad didn't let her take her van, she rode with J and Angelica. They were very early and saw Roman reading on the front steps.

"Hey, dork!" Rose called to him.

Roman looked up annoyed, then shocked, "Rose! I didn't expect you to be at school today! How are you?"

"Don't make a big deal out of it, I just want to stay busy so I don't dwell on anything, okay? Only my close friends know so let's keep it that way?"

"Oh, okay, sure. Sorry. Hey, I told Mr. Henderson yesterday I did want the part, the lead, that is. I had a really good conversation with the grad students about their process, too. I added them on Instagram and read more about the initiative they are a part of for revitalizing stories. I bet they're here if you want to go talk to them, too?" Roman rambled on, like he did when he was nervous and wanted to put others at ease.

J smiled and looked at Rose expectantly, she smiled back and nodded. The three walked around to the theater and went in. Candice was there, as was Mr. Henderson, but he was busy with a few of his advanced drama students going over their volunteer portfolios. Brendan had classes on Wednesdays, but would be on campus on Mondays and Fridays.

There was a small conference table in Mr. Henderson's office so the four squeezed in there to have a little talk.

"So I bet you two are wondering what the final cast list is, aren't you?" Candice beamed with excitement.

"Oh, yes, I mean, Roman already told us he is going to be the prince. I guess we forgot there are other people in class and other roles to be had." J laughed, she wasn't expecting to be on the list at all.

And she wasn't. Not for a lead role, at least. She was understudy for the role of the princess's watchman. She was a part of the stage crew and was relieved to be in a way.

"I, I got the part?" Rose stammered looking up and down from the cast list in front of her.

"You did! You're going to be our Turandot! Or rather, our Nasrin-Nush. Out of all the students in class you have a very commanding presence and you ran your monologue flawlessly!" Candice was startled when Rose started crying and laughing at the same time.

"It's been a rough couple of weeks for her, I don't think we expected any of this," J explained.

"Don't talk to the rest of the class yet, we are going to post this at the beginning of class today and start planning costumes and set design. There is so much to be done before the April performance. You guys are going to do great!" Candice smiled at the three high schoolers and couldn't believe how far she had come to this point. She asked them, "So, do you have time to talk about how this project got started?"

The three nodded and settled in to listen.

"I always loved history, stories, and poetry. I really believe people are more the same than different and even through time we can relate to our ancestors and future generations. I met Brendan in my undergrad studies and he is a theater major. I am a history major and we both knew of the opera Turandot and that led to us wanting to know more about where the story had come from.

A program was started at the college for multicultural stories and it was a think tank on how to bring back some more obscure tales. Most kids have been taught The Odyssey, Gilgamesh, Aeneid, Beowulf, Divine Comedy, and so on, but those are predominantly from Western Civilization so we were looking for stories from across other parts of the world.

Once all of the participants had come with stories, we were tasked in finding a way to make them more accessible to modern audiences, especially younger people, who would bring them into the spotlight. Brendan helped me adapt the original story from Haft Peykar into a play, blending it with the other adaptations, until we had the script for the play we will perform. We all studied what made the different stories unique and what made them so integral to the human experience. All civilizations wrestle with philosophy and morality.

Looking at Nizami Ganjavi's life was rewarding in and of itself. It was illuminating to learn about a Persian writer that wrote epic poems for different rulers, yet never lived a life at court. Haft Peykar is a twelfth century work that holds moralistic lessons and is a model for the earliest multiculturalism. The princesses from this poem are Indian, Turkestanian, Kazakhstan, Kievan-Rus, Moroccan, Roman, and Persian. I love Nasrin-Nush's story because it emphasizes her independence, agency, and power. It could be taken as a feminist story because she is in control of her destiny. Turandot is good for what it is, but it does take away the message that Nizami Ganjavi was trying to teach. Maybe if Puccini hadn't died the ending would have been different. I'm actually relieved that you are all so invested. You aren't that much younger than I am, so I want to be respectful and treat you as equals, but high school is such a different game than university. I wasn't sure if what we are trying to do would tap into a kid's interest."

"Well, we have been told we aren't typical teenagers. This guy over here was born an old man, I should know, I've known him since I was born." Julianna jabbed her thumb towards Roman who only slightly scowled.

"I think, the more you treat someone with respect and spend time with them, the more buy-in they have for a project. Thank you for taking the time to talk with us." Roman was much more at ease than he had been Monday afternoon.

"What changed your mind, Roman? Why did you decide to go for it?" Rose was still shocked she landed the role of Nasrin-Nush, and relieved she would get to work alongside her friend.

"Mr. Henderson talked to me. How good this would look on top of all of my other efforts. How many college applicants get to add academics, athletics, and a once in a lifetime chance to be the first lead of a brand new play? It's too good to pass up. The professors and theater buffs that are involved in this have some pretty good connections and I still don't know where I want to go to university. Also, Mercutio said it was meant to be and J, you added a good guilt trip for it being my duty to take the role for the school."

"Did you tell your mom?" Julianna asked teasingly.

"Yeah, she was a little overwhelmed by all of the other stuff going on with you guys, so it was a nice cushion to distract her with."

"Well, I could always teach you to play an instrument and you could add that to your accolades, Roman. How about an accordion?" Julianna offered mildly threateningly.

"No way! I am well out of my comfort zone already! If you're looking for a project, why don't you find some authentic instruments you can play for the play!" Roman meant that as a threat, not a challenge, but Julianna beamed as Candice looked across the table.

"Oh, do you play an instrument?" Candice asked excitedly.

"AN instrument? I haven't met an instrument I can't play, yet!" Julianna bragged.

"Yeah she has," Rose started to disclose how talented and successful Julianna already was when she got her shin kicked under the table.

"Don't bore her with any of that, Rose. Candice, let's talk during study hall after school today if you can? I'll bring some music?"

The bell rang and Candice handed J her card so they could email before they met up. The kids hopped up and left to make it to first period on time. After an emotional month and a lot of low points things were finally starting to feel like they were coming around.

15 Romeo

Wednesday passed uneventfully. Roman had been glad to see Rose and J doing alright. It had been unnerving to miss them at school on Tuesday, and then to be called out of class to talk with a police officer. He gave his side of the story and a little history of the relationship he had had with Tyler and Rose. Mercutio was called in for questioning as well, but wasn't much help for what had taken place at the party. The video of the parking lot caught a group of kids messing with his Jeep, but no one could be made out clearly. The timestamp did make it out to be right after Charles had confronted Tyler and run him off. Circumstantial at best, but still better than nothing. Rose wouldn't have to go back home, even if nothing happened to Tyler or their parents.

Drama time came around and Mr. Henderson passed out the cast list. The class was abuzz with excitement and it was more of a free day to discuss who was playing who, who were understudies, and delegating jobs of how to get all of the sets and costumes designed. In their immediate group Sloane and J were stagehands. Roman and Rose were the leads, but Bethany was the watchman that was to guard Nasrin-Nush. Sloane was understudy for the role of the princess' father King Mikhail. Class flew by and all of the confusion and apprehension from Monday was replaced with enthusiasm and vigor.

Roman took the time to finish highlighting his lines in his script during basketball practice. His teammates were pretty supportive, but made it clear it better not distract him from helping them win. They might make it to state this year if everything worked out. College scouts had been making the rounds at games and everyone on the team was hyped up.

Brendan and Candice had shown Roman and Rose how to play an ancient game called Mills or Nine Men's Morris. Part of the play had a competition of the game between Prince Bjorn and Princess Nasrin-Nush. Roman enjoyed the game so much he made his own board out of card stock and got some chips to play whenever he had free time. His parents and friends were over his obsession and it was a good distraction between everything that kept him busy. He actually wound up researching the game, which led to learning more about game theory, and how such an old and simple game can be so complex. He downloaded an app on his phone and found a website online to play the game with even more people. It was no surprise that the entire school watched such a popular guy tune out everything except a simple game that it spread like wildfire. A school club even started up to play weekly after school, but sadly Roman was too busy to attend.

Once he got home Roman reread the historical preface and got to work comparing King Bahram Gur to Prince Calaf in Turandot and Prince Calaf in Prince Calaf and the Princess of China. This was like a game of Telephone, where everyone sits in a circle and whispers a word or phrase and by the end it is totally different. Candice and Brendan really went back to the story from Haft Peykar for this play. The French and Italian adaptations made it a lot more ruthless and bloody than the original had been. While he didn't have the time to immerse himself into each incarnation of the story like Rose was doing, he did some research about how the prince had evolved through the ages and what his motivations were to marry the princess each time. Marriage and princesses were the furthest things from Roman's mind. Being successful and able to help others within the best of his abilities were what he really cared about. He was a fiercely independent person and didn't want to make someone else suffer from his ambitious nature. If love was meant for him, it would happen when he met the right person and they clicked. No sooner and no later. It was so low on his list of priorities in real life that leading as a love interest seemed unnatural at first.

However, the first time he read through the play it clicked with him. Everything made perfect sense and it was as if it were destiny, even though Mercutio had been being sarcastic. Ever since the party Mercutio seemed very standoffish and bitter. Getting questioned by the police had only made his mood more sullen and he was devastated by what Rose was going through. He had driven Roman home Tuesday night and vented, saying if he saw Tyler he would beat him to death. Rose shouldn't have to suffer because Tyler has some sociopathic inferiority complex. Roman did his best to calm Mercutio down, but he could tell he was still seething underneath. Mercutio was on a strict schedule from his parents and any trip ups would mean losing his car keys, phone, and allowance. That wasn't helping his mood, either.

That schedule left little opportunity for Mercutio to run into Tyler. Not that anyone had seen very much of him since the party. As far as the group knew the police were still looking for him to question and Rose's parents hadn't heard from him. Good riddance, thought Roman, maybe he got abducted by aliens and they would keep him. Wishful thinking rarely came true, though.

Roman heard his mom come home late, this was the later night she worked at the restaurant. Dad had been home watching the news and putting together video clip vignettes for his course. They were talking about the opioid crisis as he came out of his room to see them.

"Another one this week. That makes three that have quit because they either show up high or can't show up at all! All we need are reliable employees. I swear we should only hire family from now on." Valerie was putting away her things in a huff by the door as she spoke. Esteban got up and followed her into the kitchen and Roman followed his parents.

"Honey, I know it's hard, but we have a family that is only so big. Everyone is so busy and the restaurant is very popular. It's a staple in the town and everyone loves it. Don't worry, go take a bath and read a book, okay dear?" Esteban felt guilty because Valerie had taken a job in his family's restaurant when they were younger to make ends meet. She did eventually earn her degree in culinary arts and was very talented. She was descended from white, Anglo-Saxon Protestants so it always chagrined her that outsiders didn't think she could be an authentic Cuban chef. Everything she had learned was from Esteban's mother and grandmother. They treated her as one of their own and as they both had passed their family restaurant had become her greatest passion.

"Our town is small and the families used to be closer. Responsible adults, people our age, people we've grown up with, are getting addicted to this shit and dying. Or losing their children. I hate it! I am so frustrated and helpless. Did you know they are starting to put emergency narcan around town just like the AED machine at the mall? That's how bad it is."

"I know sweetheart, I know, it's been one of the biggest topics in my course for the past few semesters and only getting more so. The only thing we can do is advocate for better drug treatments for those suffering. Education and advocacy will turn the tide."

Roman had gotten a beer for his mom and rubbed her back with his hand. She smiled at him and patted his cheek.

"I, I was really worried that Rose was given something worse. Like fentanyl. What she got wasn't anywhere as bad as that. I hate that they like to go to parties. My friends. I'm scared because Rose and I were drinking sodas. We don't do drugs, I mean, I know Mercutio and his friends have smoked pot, but that's about it. It's scary thinking that you can avoid drugs and still, still get affected by it. It's insidious."

Valerie gave him a big hug, "Oh sweetie, it's okay. You guys were very lucky. I'm sorry you didn't feel like you could talk to us."

"It wasn't that. I wanted to talk to you guys, but Sloane got his mom there and she took care of everything. Rose and J were scared of Rose's parents. I can't believe they kicked her out. I can't believe they would put an asshole like Tyler above their daughter who is just such a good person. It isn't fair. I'm lucky to not have any siblings and to have parents as good as the both of you."

Esteban and Valerie smiled. They knew they were the lucky ones that got a son who had a naturally solid head on his shoulders.

16 Juliet

The week passed and soon it was the short week for Thanksgiving. The school district had modified the schedule to have the Wednesday before off to give people time to travel. It was nice to have the extra day to prep all of the cooking.

Valerie and Angelica hadn't had a Thanksgiving together in years. They decided on Valerie's house and made the best American, Jewish, Vietnamese, and Cuban Thanksgiving feast anyone had ever seen. Angelica had a few new recipes thanks to her time traveling overseas. They invited Sloane and Mercutio's family to dinner and it was good to have the house full of friendly faces.

Football was watched, food was eaten, and board games were played. The kids rehearsed lines for some of the funnier scenes in the play to entertain the parents. Everyone humored Roman and played Mills throughout the day, taking turns to play against the winner. Angelica and Esteban were actually the ones that seemed to be the best at the game. Time passed quickly and it was time to go home. It was also time for Rose to have to go to court and face her parents the next day. They drove back home and Angelica went upstairs to work on some invoices from holiday sales from the gallery.

Since both of the girls were hanging out in the living room, Charles got out some photo albums and sat down with them.

"We have to do a hard thing tomorrow, but it will turn out alright and I want you both to remember that you are very strong and very brave. That's something that is very true for our family." Charles flipped through the familiar photos as he spoke. Showing pictures of his mother and her parents that had managed to escape Vietnam and find a life here in America.

"You know that my mom, your grandma, married into a Catholic Irish family. Her family left Vietnam because they were Catholic. Grandpa's family worked helping the immigrants learn English and get assimilated into American life. They only had me and Aly for kids and we grew up pretty close. Aly was older than me and got a lot more interested in our Vietnamese side of the family than our Irish side. I've always held both sides close, but she married Will through some mutual Vietnamese friends."

The girls knew all of this. It was comforting to see family pictures and hear the stories again.

"Will and Aly have had a rough marriage, and I hate that you and Tyler have had to suffer because of it, Rose. I'm also sorry I haven't been a better uncle to both of you. My hands were tied and a lot of the time things had come to pass and been settled before I even heard about it wherever I was stationed."

"What do you mean, Dad?" J asked, confused.

"He means when we had to go to foster care. Tyler told a school counselor about how Dad would hit him with an electrical cord and we were in a foster home for a few months. It was right after you guys left town." Rose said quietly. Her and Tyler had vowed to never mention it.

"We've tried to get Aly to leave Will, but she won't. We tried to get custody of you kids, but we were overseas and they jumped through all of the hoops that child protective services put up. After I got home I really thought things had changed for the better, that we were going to finally have a good normal, but that wasn't what happened. They just got better at hiding it. Different people have made different calls over the years and unfortunately they got better and better at hiding the abuse and making excuses. Most people in town have a very good opinion of my sister and her husband."

J was stunned. She never knew Rose and Tyler had lived like that. How many times had she been over there, but never allowed to spend the night? She could barely remember a time when being around Tyler was pleasant and not a nightmare and sufferable experience. Her aunt and uncle pushed their kids, but abuse? She was astonished.

"We were the perfect family and had to do whatever Dad said. If he said jump, you asked how high, and even if you complied it still wasn't good enough. He focused more on Tyler because I'm 'just a girl' and should 'just get married'. I convinced him I should work as a nurse so I could eventually marry a doctor and not have to work. I want to be a doctor, though, and I want to have my own career. I kept that part to myself."

"You can do and be whatever you want as long as you work hard and stay focused," Charles patted her shoulder, "You're strong, and I'm going to be there for you, both of you, like I couldn't be for Aly. She was the big sister, how was I supposed to know any better? I take people at face value and never really worry about any dark secrets or ulterior motives. Let's get to bed, while most people are going to be fighting over getting the best deal on TVs, we are going to be seeing a judge and getting your stuff back, dear."

Morning came quickly and the grey November sky hung thickly in the air. Everyone was dressed modestly and appropriately for the hearing. Angelica and Charles were awarded guardianship and a list of belongings were agreed upon by both parties. Charles would go over to the house while just Aly was there and gather up Rose's things. Rose stared at her lap and would not look at either of her parents. Her father tried to say that the van was his, and in his name, but Angelica had gotten copies of the records from the motor vehicle department that proved otherwise. It was going to be fantastic to have her van back. Rose could feel her father's piercing gaze into her skull.

No one had seen or heard from Tyler. It was as if he put himself in a self imposed exile. It was as unsettling as it was relieving to not have to face him in court. The order of protection passed and it meant that Rose's parents and brother couldn't get within 100 feet of her, the school, or the clinic she was interning at. They were also not to email, call, or otherwise try to contact J's family. It would last until Rose was 18 and there would be another hearing at that time to see about reinstating it.

Charles had an army buddy go with him to gather Rose's belongings and drive the van back to his house. He hardly spoke to his sister while at their house. Everything was exactly as Rose had left it and they hadn't done anything with her things. Having the police go there right away and making it clear that there would be consequences if her belongings were destroyed in retaliation made a huge difference.

There were plenty of leftovers from Valerie's kitchen from the day before and the four worked hard at setting the guest room up as a permanent room for Rose. The girls spent the rest of the weekend practicing and planning for the play. J had a steel drum performance coming up in December and they sent out some evites to get people to attend. For the first time in years Rose felt safe, validated, and loved for being who she was.

17 Romeo

The weeks had passed and first semester was closing seamlessly. Verona High had made it to the playoffs for basketball, but they weren't able to make it all the way to state. It was disappointing, but with how stressful this year had been Roman was secretly relieved. He loved sports and athletics, but just because it was something he could do that he excelled at doing. Competition and being the best was never the end goal. Winning was nice, but it was more about being able to control his body and think fast while on the court around his team and the opponents.

He dressed up with his parents and went to the steel drum performance in the school auditorium. While he hadn't been that excited to go in the first place, he knew J was very excited to be on stage with the other students. She had gone to all of his basketball games with her parents, so it was the least he could do to attend her one concert. The band wore Hawaiian shirts with Santa hats and played a variety of music. It was completely different and not at all what he had expected to hear going into the concert, and leaving he was finding he had a new appreciation for what he had previously considered "garbage can music".

After the concert they went out to their favorite Italian restaurant to celebrate. Rose had been living with her aunt and uncle for over a month now and it wasn't even strange. J and Rose were like two sisters more than cousins and having both of them to talk to made it a little less awkward. J's mom didn't drop as many hints about them dating if Rose was around, but nothing stopped his mom from making sure they sat next to each other at the restaurant and shooting glances at him to be polite and pay extra attention to her. It made him so uncomfortable because he didn't feel that way about anyone, least of all J, and didn't want to lead her on. He also desperately wanted to keep the peace with his mother.

Roman's dad and Charles both talked about football and the upcoming Super Bowl party Charles was going to be hosting. The moms were talking about Christmas and the holidays. All three of the kids kept bouncing back and forth between both of the conversations while also gossiping and discussing everything that had been going on around the school.

"I am so ready for a break! This high school stuff is next level, I can't remember the last time I had to work so hard and was so busy. I love it, but getting to spend some time being lazy and playing some video games is a welcomed change," J smiled before she started stuffing her mouth with bites of spaghetti.

"Enjoy it while it lasts, second semester is high school hard mode. First semester even the teachers are still getting acclimated to what is going on," Rose was taking neat and deliberate bites of her salad, "How about you, Roman, are you taking extra classes so you don't get bored over the break?"

Roman smiled at Rose's teasing, "No, Rose, actually I'm excited for a bit of a break myself. I was wondering if you still wanted to get together to practice the play like we've been doing. Oh, and Sloane and Mercutio want us to come over. Sloane's been writing a campaign for Shadowrun he wants all of us to try out, he was thinking of inviting Bethany, too. Would the Friday after Christmas work for you guys?"

The girls looked at each other and agreed that would work out perfectly.

Roman's grandparents, aunts and uncles, and some cousins came to town for Christmas and he got a ton of gifts. A new laptop, some shoes he had been hoping for, new clothes, and a pass for driving lessons from his mom for when he was "ready". After dinner the family spent time playing party video games and doing a white elephant gift exchange. Roman's favorite was a plastic saran wrap ball his aunt made every year filled with toys, candy, gift cards, and other prizes. Everyone sat in a circle and one person held a bowl with two dice in it. The person next to them held and tried to unwrap the saran wrap ball as quickly as possible while the person with the bowl rolled the dice until they hit doubles. That signaled the ball being passed around until the last person got the grand prize in the middle. As everyone finally started going home Roman got a little wistful helping his parents clean up. This time next year he would be coming home from his first semester of college and he still hadn't decided on where he was going to go or what exactly to major in. Would he be any more decisive in twelve months time, or would he still feel uncertain about how life should play out?

Friday rolled around and Rose picked him up to go over to Mercutio and Sloane's for Shadowrun. Mom had gotten all the best snacks and drinks for the kids and they went straight down to the basement to play. J and Bethany were completely new to tabletop gaming so Sloane had met with them a few days earlier to help them make their characters. The goal of the party was to infiltrate and try and take down a corporation that was trying to turn people into mindless zombie drones to control the world. Everyone had fun and they made plans to play every week on Sunday after school started. Sloane was so happy it all went well.

"Oh, before you guys leave, I have to ask. Would your parents be cool if we have a sleepover for New Years? Just us, no one else, no alcohol, my parents will be here. They can call my mom if they have any questions."

"I'm down," Roman said.

"I should be able to, but I'll have to check," Bethany said.

"We'll ask," J said looking at Rose who wasn't ready to commit, "Give us a few days to get back to you, okay?"

Rose reached out and squeezed J's hand as a thank you. Roman was oblivious of that, or why they would be apprehensive about coming over. He was looking forward to a junk food night of bad movies and even worse games.

18 Juliet

J wasn't worried about going over to Mercutio and Sloane's place. She was pretty sure her parents would even give her the okay, especially her mom, after she found out that Roman would be attending. Rose had been having some pretty intense anxiety since going to court. Her family hadn't contacted her and she hadn't heard anything about Tyler. Going out to the mall, grocery shopping, or even out to eat was a little nerve racking for her. Her parents were homebodies and didn't go out anywhere very much, she avoided the few places they did go. It was more the threat of randomly running into Tyler that gave her the biggest panic attacks.

The girls talked and weighed the pros and cons of going out. They deserved to have some fun and some down time, it would just be close friends, and their parents might say they weren't allowed to go anyhow.

"How about this, if you feel stressed out and want to leave we leave. No matter what. You give me a sign and I'll act like I need to puke my guts out and you have to take me home. That way it isn't on you, okay?" J was hanging upside down from the edge of her bed.

"I don't know, J, maybe you should just go on your own. I can stay in and hang out with your mom and dad and do some reading," Rose fiddled with her hands nervously.

"I'm not ditching you. Unless you want to get rid of me because I'm a pest. Other than that it's you and me, okay?" J put her hands on the floor and flipped herself backwards onto her feet as she spoke.

"No, no it's not that! Be careful! Let's go, let's try it and if it gets too bad I'll ask you if you think the tuna fish went bad," Rose started to say.

"And I'll say, "Oh no! I think I'm going to be sick" and we can go!" J finished.

The parents gave their blessings, they were actually excited because they had been invited to a party at a resort through some friends of Angelica's at the gallery. Valerie and Esteban would be joining them, too, so it was good that Roman didn't have to spend New Year's Eve alone in the house. The girls let the parents know they would update them if they left Sloane and Mercutio's to come home. Both sides argued over if the girls should stay home alone if it came to that. The girls kept telling the parents to stay and have a good time, they could take care of themselves, but the parents kept insisting if it came to them having to leave that the girls were more important than some resort party and they'd take a Lyft home.

Everyone arrived in the early evening with pillows, sleeping bags, and more junk food to add to the copious amount of snacks that were already spread out and provided. Sloane and Mercutio's parents had some friends over to watch old movies upstairs and the kids took over the basement. They ran some of the Shadowrun campaign for a few hours, took a pizza break, and then went outside to shoot off some fireworks.

When they got back inside Rose, Mercutio, and Bethany put on a movie to make fun of and Sloane joined J on the couch under the stairs down to the basement. Roman had stayed outside to clean up fireworks and enjoy the crisp, cold night. As the movie went on Sloane and J slowly got closer together. Two hands slowly slid across the couch and began to touch when Sloane made his move to wrap her fingers in his. After a few moments J slid down to rest her head on Sloane's chest and he put his arm around her and they shared a blanket.

Her hair smelled amazing and was so beautiful and shiny. He stroked the strands gently out of her face and behind her ear. J smiled up at him and snuggled in closer, squeezing a knee with her hand. The movie ended and Rose, Bethany, and Mercutio got some snacks before starting another one, not wanting to disturb their friends.

Sloane leaned down when they were alone and gently kissed J chastly on the lips. She returned the kiss, first slowly parting her lips, and then wider they began to kiss more deeply. As they broke the kiss J slid away and put her hands in her face and Sloane got worried.

"Are you okay, I am so sorry, if that was too forward or too fast I'm sorry!"

"No, you're fine Sloane, really. I really, really like you. A lot. Before I moved back home I moved too fast with other guys and, well, I got them in trouble. I don't want to get you in trouble. I want to do things right when and if I'm ready to have a partner."

Sloane beamed and gave J a hug as he answered her, "Don't worry at all, I really like you, too, since the first time I saw you! I spent a ton of time being really shy around you when I'm not normally like that. You aren't going to get me into trouble, making sure you are happy and comfortable are my top priorities first and foremost."

J smiled back at him, but stood up, "That means a lot to me, it really does. I need some air for a minute, though, I'm going to step back outside. I'll be right back, okay?"

"Oh, uh, oh. Okay. I'll be here if you need anything, okay? I'll go upstairs and make some cocoa, would you like cocoa."

"That sounds delicious!"

J slid the door firmly behind her and tightened her scarf and jacket around her against the cold. It really was a beautiful night and she briefly wondered how her parents were doing. They had messaged at midnight and she sent a quick message back letting them know everything was going great. It absolutely was, she had been hoping that Sloane would make a move tonight because she had been dropping hints like crazy. With her other boyfriends she had always made the first move and was too rash, too hasty. Moving home, adjusting to the high school life, and supporting Rose had taken a lot of her focus away from thinking about dating anyone. Sloane was so sweet and she absolutely loved his brother and parents. The only thing she had to consider was how her mother would react when she was so dead set on her dating...

"Roman!"

As J had walked around she came to the front of the house where there was a porch swing. She totally forgot that Roman was here, much less still outside. He was sitting on the swing in the middle with his arms across the back wide just looking up at the stars. He smiled and slid over making room for her. Crap. Crap, crap, crap, crap! J thought furiously. It would be a jerk move to turn around and run back inside and she really wasn't ready to do that, but she really had been hoping on being alone, too. Reluctantly she went up to the swing and took a seat and looked up to where Roman had been looking.

"I didn't realize you were still out here, what on earth are you doing?"

"Oh. I was just looking at the constellations. Mercutio's porch is just right for stargazing and look, you can see Orion and Taurus really well." Roman pulled out his phone that was opened to a sky map app and showed her, "And the International Space Station will be flying over any minute now. I felt like I should sit out here and wave to the astronauts. Wish them a Happy New Year, too. That's probably pretty silly, though."

J was a little stunned, in a sweet way. Roman was pretty cold and gruff towards her, and his charisma and good boy act always felt artificial to her so she really couldn't respect him. The past year had taught her a lot about her childhood friend and she was getting a new appreciation for him. Oh man. If he found out Sloane and her had kissed would he be devastated? She didn't want to ruin his night, but she had to nip his crush in the bud so it didn't fully bloom into an infatuation.

Before she could start he suddenly pointed, "Look! Up there, do you see that light, it kind of looks like a plane but will move really straight and kind of fast across the sky." J followed Roman off the swing into the yard as he waved wildly at the little light hundreds of miles above them. She joined him and it made her laugh. Once it was gone they walked back to the swing.

"Are you warm enough? Do you want my jacket?" Roman asked her with genuine concern.

"Oh, no, no I'm fine, I'm about ready to go back inside. Look. We've got to talk though and I need to tell you something important."

Roman sat up straighter and scooted ever so slightly away. It wouldn't be an exaggeration to call his motion a recoil.

"J wait, I don't want you to be upset and I should have spoken to you earlier before it got too far."

"Upset? Why wouldn't I be upset? You're not a bad guy, but I really think it would be for the best," before she could finish Roman uncharacteristically cut her off mid sentence.

"No, no, I think if we started dating it would be for the worst. I've been too scared to say anything to you because I just can't believe that you would really be infatuated with me. I get so uncomfortable and freaked out every time my mom tells me how much you are into me."

"ME into YOU?!" J stood up and the swing swayed wildly, "Why on earth would I be infatuated with you?! My mom said that YOU are in love with ME!"

"WHAT?!"

"WHAT!"

They were now both standing and staring at each other wide eyed as they put the pieces together. Their moms had been conspiring behind their backs to make them go out because they wanted them to date. This whole time they had been fake polite to each other out of fear of breaking the other's heart.

"So... you DON'T like me like that?" Roman asked

"God no, you're like an old man, no offense," J said with a shiver, "You mean you aren't infatuated with me?"

"Of course not! I don't even really like... anybody. I don't know if I should tell you this, but Mercutio thinks Sloane really likes you." Roman was not used to discussing relationships and crushes. He had no idea if he was helping Sloane or violating his confidence. J sat back down on the swing slowly.

"Yeah, I know Sloane likes me. That's why I was out here actually, we kissed at midnight." J smiled at Roman as he sat down.

"Oh! Oh wow. Why aren't you in there with him? I feel like I'm interrupting you if you wanted to be alone you could have just let me know and I would have gone inside." Roman would have kept stammering if J hadn't waved her arms and interrupted him.

"Roman! Roman, chill, it's fine, I just wanted some fresh air and to think things through. I came back home to start fresh and really take everything in slowly and deliberately. I really like Sloane and I don't want to mess anything up. Don't worry, I mostly was thinking of how you would feel if I started dating him. Who do you like?"

The silence and pause hung in the air thickly. Roman looked down at his hands and fidgeted nervously.

"I, I don't think that I have ever really liked someone. I don't, I don't get a feeling of wanting to kiss or even worse get more physical with anyone. I think something went wrong with me. I feel really bad that I can't reciprocate those feelings for Rose because she is absolutely outstanding. Maybe I haven't met the right person, but I really don't feel like I need to go out and find someone. I'm really happy by myself and it is annoying how everyone thinks that they need to fix that about me."

"You are NOT broken. You are you and you are a wonderful guy. Come here." J leaned over, kneeling on the swing and gave Roman a big hug that he returned and started to cry. J started to cry, too. They weren't even sad, it was just an excess of pent up emotion between the two of them. This whole first semester had been so stressful and so awkward. They were seeing each other as adversaries to avoid, but stupid fate kept flinging them together. Oh when they saw their mothers again they were going to have to set some things very clear and explicit.

Roman and J went back inside together and Sloane was as good as his word at having some cocoa for J. He tilted his head like a puppy as she sat down at the game table in his lap and she smiled and nodded as she took the mug from him and sipped at it. It had been so long the marshmallows had melted into a delicious, creamy layer of froth. Sloane looked over at Roman questioningly and Roman just smiled and shrugged. The kids played card games, board games, watched more movies, played some fighting games until slowly they fell asleep in the early morning.

19 Romeo

There wasn't much more to be said about the last days of winter break before Roman went back to school. He was surprised, happy, and relieved to have talked things out with Julianna. That sense of peace didn't follow over to his mother, who still was needling him to make "more of an effort" despite Roman explaining in excruciating detail that Julianna was dating Sloane. Valerie didn't seem to worry about that one bit. After that, Julianna was mostly out of sight and out of mind for Roman.

He had received his acceptance letters to the many universities he had applied to and had settled on Cornell. January through February he would have to fill out paperwork and get set to actually enroll. The school and his family were making a big deal out of it. Checking all the boxes brought Roman a great sense of accomplishment. Since his family made less than sixty thousand per year he qualified for a free ride to the prestigious university. The school doesn't offer athletic or academic scholarships, but rather will support the students with the most drive from the neediest families. This suited Roman perfectly. The only thing that was still bothering him was that he hadn't decided on a major. How on earth was he supposed to narrow down the rest of his life to one specific interest?

Knowing he was already accepted to college next year and was sure to graduate didn't make it any more difficult for him to work towards his goals. He was buckling down and became even more determined. The absolute lack of senioritis was completely obnoxious to just about everyone around him, even his teachers.

The one and only class it was appreciated in was theater and that drive to have a great performance thrust him headlong into memorizing his lines. That was easy, he was ahead of the rest of the class in terms of being ready to perform. He didn't realize it, but he had become so familiar with the script that he had memorized most of the play itself and most of his free time was spent in reflecting on the intricacies of the plot and could imagine the scenes in his mind.

The play was in March and class time was spent rehearsing, designing the set, and creating props. Julianna's mom had volunteered to help create some of the costumes. Local costume and fabric shops sponsored the school with donations of items they didn't need anymore so there were some pretty choice items available for the play. Candice had a few other college students who were joining in on the think tank help write some music for the play itself. Julianna spent a lot of time working with that group and with the group who was creating the props. The think tank had gathered some of the cultural clubs from campus to support the music in the play and use authentic instruments and keep every facet of the play respectful and true to the cultures being included.

Roman supported the other cast members and the understudies in practicing scenes and rehearsing the lines. Brendan helped those students out and the entire thing was coming together nicely. The entire class had a business and buzz about it that was very satisfying.

"Hey Roman, did you get asked to the dance, yet?" Sloane asked him in between scenes.

"What? Oh. Yeah I kind of forgot about it. Nobody has asked me, and that's okay. I'm going to be volunteering to help set it up and work with the DJ and snack table. That's more fun anyway," Roman explained.

Every year the school had a Sadie Hawkins style dance after winter break instead of a winter formal. They had decided more dances through the year was just a little too complicated and combining them resulted in the best turn out. Prom was held in May and was the last event of the year. Roman never went to the other dances, except for junior prom the year before, and only due to his mother's pestering about it being a rite of passage. Mercutio gave him the idea that if he was too busy working a dance, he wouldn't have to find a date to actually attend a dance.

Sloane kind of swayed waiting for Roman to ask him if he had been asked to the dance by anyone, but his mind was on the play. He finally interjected, "J asked me! It was so great that she was able to go to my house on New Years. I didn't know if you had heard if Rose had asked anyone at all."

"No, Sloane, I hadn't spoken with them really since the New Years. I imagine she will ask someone if she wants to go, but if she doesn't that's alright, too. I don't make a big deal out of dances."

Sloane nodded and took the hint that Roman was more concerned with getting the work done than gossiping about girls. In another month they would have a few dress rehearsals and spend some time in class going through the play to see where the weak parts were so the next month could be focused on tightening those parts up. Students that weren't in theater were very confused about the play and so were the large majority of the teachers. That didn't bother the drama kids one bit, it was so exciting to be doing something that had never been done before.

The weekend brought the Sadie Hawkins dance and it was a hoedown theme. Roman helped the student council go all out in constructing a fake wagon with hay bales for a photo booth spot, decorating the gym to look like a barn, and placing fake animals around the sides. He heard that Tyler's band was originally hired to play the venue, but had been switched out for a regular DJ. Sloane showed up with J, but Mercutio and Rose never showed up. Roman started the night out front taking student's tickets and directing them to the photo spot.

"Hey! Alright, look at you two!" Roman beamed as he greeted his friends, getting up from the table to give J and Sloane a big hug.

They were both dressed to match the theme. Sloane had light blue jeans, boots, and a checkered shirt tucked into his pants. He even had a white cowboy hat on and if Roman hadn't known him his entire life he would've been certain he could have been a real cowboy. J was wearing a matching checkered shirt, but wore a pair of darker blue overalls with a black cowboy hat. It had silver studs accenting the hat band and she looked like she walked right out of a photoshoot for a western themed magazine. It made Roman happy to see them together and was a relief he didn't have to worry about his mom's nagging insistence on him getting a girlfriend.

After about a half an hour the group taking tickets cleaned up the table and went inside to check out the festivities for themselves. Most of the music was the regular, contemporary school dance music that teenagers love, but every five songs or so a country themed one came on and the kids goofed off trying to pretend to square dance. The teacher chaperones actually led a few line dances and the PE teachers had done a few weeks of dance each year. Roman caught his own foot tapping and he actually joined in for the <u>Boot Scootin' Boogie</u>. He smiled to himself and wondered why he had always been so down and negative on school events like this before. If he had talked to his junior year self at the same time last year and told him one small part of how wild this year had been he wouldn't have believed a word.

He went over and talked with Sloane and J. They had gotten a ride with Rose who was going to pick them back up. It didn't take long for Roman to message his mom that he would catch a ride back home with his friends.

"So, how did you like your first high school dance, J?" Roman asked her as they waited on the front steps for Rose to get there.

"It was fantastic! Way better than any middle school dance I'd ever attended. Of course, I think that the main draw was that of my lovely date here." J patted Sloane's arm as they stood waiting to which he blushed furiously.

"It was fun, probably even more fun than prom last year," Roman agreed, "But don't tell Rose that. I had a great time with her, but it's nicer for me to just organize and watch rather than be in attendance."

They stopped at an all night diner after Rose picked them up. They ordered appetizers and coffee. This particular restaurant had fun board games and they spent some time playing Scrabble and Uno. A few other kids from school were there, too, and it was a nice way to end the evening.

20 Juliet

Second semester was definitely a whirlwind, but having made it through the first half of the year Julianna was more than able to balance the challenges. Steel drum and drama was consuming all of her free time. She tried to get into theater class to work on public speaking and take a break from music, but it seemed impossible for her to completely escape it. At least working with a group of college students on different instruments and culturally varied compositions was an enjoyable change of pace. Professionally she was trained to perform classical music, personally she enjoyed classic rock and anything super bizarre or obscure. Folk and punk were where she was currently focusing on writing music, but this was highly top secret and she was not willing to divulge these experiments with anyone. Every class Julianna had a little notebook where she kept scrupulous notes on everything unique and intriguing about another culture, their music, their instruments, and the significance. It was also refreshing to play dumb and give the young adults a chance to be the teacher sometimes. No one had figured out "who" she was and she quite liked it like that.

Sloane was absolutely charming and spending time with him and chatting was definitely a big distraction. She hadn't told her mom she had a boyfriend, yet, and Rose knew to keep it on the down low. They ate lunch together, texted near constantly, and hung out as much as possible. With Angelica coming into drama class more often to check on the progress of the set design and costumes it was important that they kept their distance so she didn't figure out what was up. Julianna's parents were very realistic in terms of teenagers dating and going through puberty, but she had gotten a little too hot and heavy with some of her previous boyfriends. She hadn't gotten in trouble with her family, but she definitely got a reputation around the last base among the mothers of the kids her age. This didn't bother Angelica, she kept more in touch with her old friends back in the States than she had tried to make real friendships with the other military wives. It was still important for Julianna to make sure that her mother knew that she was mature and not rushing into anything too young. Julianna wasn't aware of it, but a lot of her mother's trepidation came from seeing Valerie having Roman so young. They weren't that far apart in age, but Angelica was at least in her twenties and married before becoming pregnant. Valerie was about four months along with Roman when she got married to Esteban, but they were one of the happiest married couples Julianna had ever seen.

Dating and having a partner really interested Julianna, but she still wasn't too sure if she wanted to get married. Being only fourteen she also was trying to be level headed and not get ahead of herself. These next few years were going to be calm and there is never any sense in growing up too fast.

It was a lot of fun to spend evenings making costumes with her mom and Rose. A few of the other students in class and people in their families were somewhat proficient in seamstress or tailoring work. Bethany came over to have her costume made and then regularly started coming over to help. As the weeks passed it was seeming more and more appropriate to fill her parents in that she was actually dating Sloane. They knew they had gone to the dance together, and that Rose decided to skip it. The hints her mom kept dropping about Roman were coming to a head and she had been saving the revelation that she and Roman knew what was up for just the right time. Little did Julianna know that Roman had told Valerie about her dating Sloane, and Valerie of course told Angelica. Since finding out she had just quietly monitored what Julianna was up to. She had all faith and trust in her daughter's choices, and was curious as to why she was keeping her boyfriend a secret.

A few days before Valentine's Day Sloane asked Julianna if she would like to go to the movies with him on a real date. She was ecstatic and decided that it had gone well and she wasn't feeling pressured or rushed. Sloane was the real deal and it was alright to let her parents know that they were an item.

"Hey Mom, Dad," Julianna said one morning at breakfast, "Remember how I went to the dance with Sloane?"

"Yes dear, you said you had a good time," her mother said while picking up the dishes from the table.

"Well I just wanted to talk to you both about how we've been dating for a while now. Valentine's Day is coming up and he asked if he could take me out to the movies and I'd like to get him something nice. I wanted to make sure it was for real and not just a silly crush before you guys got attached."

Her mom smiled at her dad and he smiled back. They had just been wondering last night if it was going to come up this way.

"Sure thing, honey, Sloane is a nice kid and his parents are great. I'm still thankful his mom was there that night for Rose when we couldn't be," her dad said, giving her a big side hug.

"Do you think I could plan a dinner for after the movie and cook with him? I'd like to make him something nice."

"What a sweet idea, J, we can go shopping for it tomorrow," her mom came over and gave her a hug too.

Rose had already excused herself from the table and was just getting out of the shower when Julianna knocked on her door to give her a heads up.

"That will be great, J! I'm so happy for you guys, I told you your parents would be cool and that you didn't have to wait to tell them. They're not like my parents, you know?"

"It wasn't that... I didn't want to move too fast with Sloane until I was sure we really clicked and it wasn't more than just infatuation. That I liked him for who he is and that he likes me for who I am. Not, y'know, who I 'am,'" and she gestured to the shelf of awards and concert pictures on a display by her closet.

"I get it, for sure," Rose agreed, "But I've known Sloane through Mercutio for a long time and they are both sweethearts. If you had asked me who I would've seen you going out with I wouldn't have been surprised. Now your mom and Roman's mom trying to get you two together? That was always ridiculous! I know they say opposites attract, but that isn't even close to a good match. Those two ladies have always been crazy!"

"Not like us, though, right?" Julianna grinned while asking her cousin.

"No, we're alright, we're cool."

"Hey, Rose? What about you? I know you went to prom with Roman, but I don't know how you really feel about him. Are you a little sad he isn't more interested?"

Rose looked out the window and pulled her hair back before answering, "Well last year I was a little upset, like he didn't like me because there was something wrong with me. Now after everything that's happened I'm glad that he isn't into me. I don't think I could handle how high maintenance he is and how much he cares about being the best at absolutely everything. He isn't even a jerk about it, though, he just is trying to challenge himself and he is like an unstoppable force. I worry about the day when he runs out of things to do. Like this play! I know how butthurt he was to get put into drama class, but have you seen what a natural he is in terms of acting? I think he might really be a robot. A nice robot, but still, there is something otherworldly about Roman at times. Everything is so effortless to him."

"He's just wired that way. You're right that he isn't trying to be better than everyone else, he just tries to always do his best. I think that most people goof off and he is always serious. That's different, but in a nice kind of different way. It's good to know you don't have feelings for him. I feel kind of bad ditching you for Sloane."

"J, it's not a problem. I'm busy with senior year stuff and figuring out what to do. I'm so thankful I can stay here, but I need to figure out college and probably get myself an apartment."

"No apartment! Stay here! Stay here forever!"

"J. When you're a senior are you going to want to keep living at home?"

"If you're here with me? Yes! You're like my cousin sister!"

"Okay, weirdo, I'll ask you that again in three years and we'll see if you still want to put up with me."

Julianna tossed a teddy bear at Rose who blocked it and grabbed a pillow. Julianna grabbed another one up and they divulged into an epic pillow fight until Angelica hollered at Julianna she had ten minutes to figure out what she wanted to get for Valentine's dinner at the store.

Julianna had most of the food prepared ahead of time. Her dad drove her and Sloane to a movie at the mall and they took some time wandering around afterwards just window shopping. He had gotten her a small teddy bear with a bouquet of flowers and she gave him a book she knew he had been waiting to come out. They went back to her house and she showed him how to cook a chicken rice bowl meal. They shared some chocolate fondue which was a really neat treat. Her mother told her that the fondue wouldn't work, that it would all burn up and be ruined, but Julianna had looked up online how to use two pots, one boiling with water underneath, to gently melt the chocolate on the top of the stove. They ate strawberries, bananas, brownies, and marshmallows until they were ready to pop! They hung out in Julianna's room for a little while afterwards to play some video games and talk, door open, of course.

They hung out with the parents and Rose for a little bit until Sloane's mom came over to pick him up. They shared a quick kiss goodbye to which nobody teased them or gave them a hard time. Julianna appreciated that. Other parents or families can really be cruel to their kids. Making them feel self conscious or wrong for trying to date and as a teenager you're already so out of place and awkward. Having supportive and loving adults was a blessing she knew she was fortunate to have all too well.

21 Romeo

March was little more than a month away and they had already completed their first dress rehearsal. Everyone knew their lines, the sets were magnificent, and the costumes were on point. The high school kids didn't realize how relieved the college kids were, they hadn't understood how the play would look at the end, but everything fit together like a puzzle. It was such complete serendipity that it was as if it was meant to be. These students and these instructors were creating something new and exciting from something old and nearly forgotten.

Roman was happy that the play was going to be over soon. He enjoyed his time in drama, and was actually freely admitting that to his mom at this point. After the play, volleyball season would be in full swing and he would get to finally finish his last sport of his high school career. It was perfect that basketball lasted first quarter, the play was soaking up second and third, and volleyball would finish up fourth. Thinking back to his meeting with Ms. Sepulveda in the summer showed him that the stress of having a performing arts class on top of his sports would be insurmountable. Time had been moving so quickly all year, but now it was running at a snail's pace. All he wanted was to be done with high school and focus on university.

Problem about university was he still had to choose a major. He really favored Cornell, but in just a few short weeks his mind had already changed and added more possibilities. It was overwhelming to have so many different choices available. He wished he had just had one that accepted him, not having a choice is way less stress than having to be decisive and know what you're going to be doing. Did he want to be close to home? Go across the country? Was basketball or volleyball more important to pursue? He still wasn't sure what major to choose, but through the year he had seen his friends have to deal with more than kids should have to put up with. He knew the world was messed up, but was paralyzed with what he could do by himself to make any sort of meaningful contribution to changing it for the better. Going into medical school he could help a few specific people, but after spending the night in the hospital with Rose he wasn't sure if that would be something his heart could handle. Plus all of the different specialities he could focus on. No, lately he had been toying with getting into law and political science. He had no desire to be a politician and work for a political campaign and run for office, but maybe he could help defend the most vulnerable people and work as a civil rights defense lawyer. He could spend his time and energy coming up with solutions to the world's problems and helping others to work as hard as he did.

After college he could go into professional sports, maybe, he had some unique promise. Sports was something he enjoyed for the fun of it and was naturally talented. It didn't seem very giving and he hated feeling greedy or selfish. Could he really stand all the drama and primadonna players that were so ruthlessly ugly and bullish. High school sports served a means to an end to help him get into a better school and not cost an exorbitant amount of money. If he didn't continue to compete in athletics through his prime would he regret wasting his youthful energy and naturally talented body. Or if he pushed too hard too soon would he have injuries and chronic pain for the rest of his life?

And then there was the acting. Although Roman knew that even in just one year he had learned that there was more out there in the world than he realized before, he still really didn't see the power and value in the arts. Everyone was really excited about him acting and the attention just made him uncomfortable. With sports there was a lot more repetition and rules and a goal. Dealing with his own emotion and feelings on stage was still raw and uncomfortable, despite being yet another thing he was apparently naturally good at.

Suddenly he was blinded by a flash in his face in the darkness of the theater.

"Beautiful, darling, beautiful! I'm going to call it "Handsome Man Brooding Alone"!" Mercutio was grinning madly with a huge camera as Roman blinked the white flashes out of his vision.

"What the hell?"

"I'm helping newspaper and yearbook get some candids of the big play! We might actually get into the local newspaper, wouldn't that be good? Get you some publicity for that gorgeous mug. I'll take the pictures and you will be my model." Mercutio had already taken some big steps back just in case Roman decided to grab for the camera.

"You show me that before you show anyone else or you're dead to me!"

"I promise you will be the first to see my developed roll, this is art, you're going to love it!" Mercutio jumped around to the stage and disappeared to take more pictures of unsuspecting victims.

A couple of thoughts ran through Roman's head. Whatever he decided to do he wanted to always be close to Mercutio and he wanted to make sure to have time for his parents. He didn't like his mom being stressed out about the restaurant all the time, but he knew that food service and culinary arts were not his strong suit. There we go, he thought wryly, one thing I can mark down that I suck at. At least with a free ride he wouldn't have to ask them for money, maybe she could cut down on her hours soon.

Up on stage J was moving some backgrounds around. Sloane was helping and they looked really happy. Roman smiled and had been a lot more easy going since they had hashed everything out. She was working with a few other musician students from their school and the college to record music for the play. Live music was an extra step they weren't going to, but it would be nice to have some fun and original music recorded by students. It wasn't very often different classes get the opportunity to collaborate on projects, but this was just more and more positivity radiating from what started off as one small high school theater course.

Roman flipped to the planner app on his phone and added a time to meet up with Mercutio, because he really had no idea what his friend's plans were. Suddenly he was fairly sheepish and ashamed for being so self absorbed. It was much easier to plan big life choices and decisions around others and those connections than to try and suss out what was real and important to him. That was wholly and entirely overwhelming. Again, Roman bitterly thought, another thing he sucked at was being decisive without external guidance. Maybe he wasn't ready to be an independent adult. Older teenagers have the disadvantage of not realizing all humans are faking it, the more an adult seems with it and put together, the bigger a faker they are.

22 Juliet

It was the week before the play. That Wednesday there would be a dress rehearsal for the middle and elementary students from nearby schools and then Thursday, Friday, and Saturday would each have a show. Their class wasn't big enough to have an A cast and B cast, but they did have understudies just in case and might even tag team switch out for some scenes. Thursday was the big show that they really were pulling for. They were going to film it and even live stream it on the high school and college website. It was a truly premiere piece for the students and their professors working on it. This was just making Julianna more content to be in the background for once.

Still, being a member of the stage crew was a huge responsibility. It was an important project, but also they were making it student focused and fun. At any point someone wasn't having fun anymore they would stop and reassess what their true goals with the project were. Candice and Brendan were very cognizant of not making the teenagers be exploited at their expense. That foundation was really central to the phenomenal feeling of the play so far.

A bunch of kids were over at Julianna's house to finish stage props that they could transport easily to school. They had ordered about twenty-five styrofoam wig heads, about a dozen toy skulls, and a smattering of old Halloween masks donated from a costume shop that needed to update its inventory. These would make up the heads on the fortress wall. A group of kids were having the best time adding clay and designing different faces for each head. The individuality of it all was really special.

Suddenly Angelica's phone rang. She looked at the number, sat the head she had been prepping down, and walked into the kitchen. Julianna slowly got up and stood by the kitchen door, but could only make out muffled voices of her mom being agitated.

"Charles! Come here please!" Angelica had opened the door to the backyard and called for Julianna's dad who was working out in the yard on some bigger backgrounds. The door closed and he took the phone. Julianna could hear her mom leave to go into the bedrooms upstairs.

"I told you, do not call me or my wife unless it is a life or death emergency. No. No! That's not our problem, that is not my family's problem. That's your son and your son's choices. I will not enable you enabling him! Absolutely not, maybe finally having some consequences for his choices might straighten him up. I don't care, it isn't my problem, don't call here again." Charles was furious like Julianna had never heard him before. It didn't take much for her to figure out that he was talking about Tyler. She couldn't tell if it was Rose's mom or dad on the other side, though. Thank goodness her dad's angry voice carried better than her mom's. She could hear his heavy feet walk upstairs. Julianna looked around and everyone was still engrossed with what they were doing so she slowly walked up the stairs behind her dad. Once she was outside of her parents' room she could barely make out what they were saying.

Words trickled out like "arrested", "police", "drugs", "bust", and "tell the girls?". Julianna didn't press her luck and almost ran straight into Rose who had just started to come look for her. Julianna grabbed Rose by the wrist and took her into the kitchen.

"I think your parents just called. Something happened with Tyler, but I couldn't make it out. I don't think they'll tell us until we're done and everyone goes home." Rose sat down and cursed as Julianna put a tea kettle on. There were pizzas and soda for all the kids who were over. The tea was just finished brewing by the time Angelica and Charles came out and they thankfully took mugs from Julianna.

"Let's finish up here, we're almost done. Sloane's mom is coming by to use her van to take everything to the school, everyone should clear out then." Angelica said and took her tea back to the living room where her prop head was waiting for her.

For Rose and Julianna it took an agonizingly long time for all the non family members to shuffle out. Sloane realized something was off and Julianna just whispered, "I'll fill you in later, don't worry." and a kiss on the cheek. Once things were straightened up the family sat down in the living room.

"So your parents called, Rose, it seems that Tyler was caught selling fentanyl. He's been arrested and can't be bailed out unless someone is willing to be responsible for keeping an eye on him." Angelica started.

"Your mom started and then your dad joined in. The police are refusing to let him go home to them since they found a huge stash of drugs in his room at their house. They wanted us to take him in here and when we explained absolutely not they are "ready" for you to apologize and come back home now for your brother." Charles had been having a hard time keeping the anger out of his voice and Angelica rubbed his shoulders.

"That's nuts. That's absolutely nuts. I want nothing to do with him! I want nothing to do with them!" Rose started panicking and Julianna grabbed her into a huge hug.

"You don't have to! Absolutely not. You're here, you're safe, and that isn't going to change. I'm sorry your parents haven't been able to give you what you need and we can't fix or change that, but we will do anything that we can for you, dear." Charles leaned over to squeeze Rose's hand.

"They're living in a fantasy land. They thought if we vouch for Tyler a judge will go easier on him, what with Charles' military service and our family's standing in our community. They're very angry, but that's on them. They also need to learn to live with the fall out from the choices they made." Angelina nodded as she stood up, "Tyler is in jail and probably will be for quite a long time. It's so sad, when he was a little boy he had the whole world ahead of him. I wish we had been closer so maybe we could've helped."

"I don't think that sort of "would've, should've" talk is going to be productive now. He's an adult and grown man. There is no excuse for him to not know right from wrong." Charles stood up with Angela.

The girls hugged the parents and everyone got ready for bed. Rose decided to bunk up with Julianna for the night and even though they were safe and Tyler was in jail they double checked all the door and window locks. As snug as sisters they eventually drifted off to sleep.

23 Romeo

That Sunday the newspaper came out with a full page feature in the arts and culture section showcasing their play. There were photos of the entire class and listed everyone by name for the parts they would have. Roman's mother was ecstatic and spent the day simultaneously bragging online and calling everyone on her contact list. At least that made it easier for Roman to slip away to the park to go practice with the rest of the cast.

Everyone was nervous, even kids who had acting experience. None of them had ever gotten involved in something this monumental. The kids couldn't talk to anyone in town without getting into a discussion about the play now. The days were going by as rapidly as falling dominos. The moment of truth was the dress rehearsal in front of the younger students on Wednesday during class. Roman was worried the theme and language of the play would leave the kids clueless and bored. They all seemed so painfully young and small. After the first act and dodging to avoid the stone guardians the kids seemed hypnotized. He didn't spend much time around little kids and had been dreading a rude and unruly group. The drama class invited the kids up to the stage in groups afterwards and gave them autographs on their programs and took pictures for the teachers to send out to their students' families.

That one little performance gave the class a huge boost of confidence and glee. There were still some butterflies, but full-on stage fright was gone. The eighth grade teacher asked for any seniors to please come in a few weeks and give a talk to the students about what high school is like and answer questions. Both Rose and Roman joyfully volunteered. Roman was truly befuddled by a group of girls that were extremely giggly and star struck by him.

Thursday night. Everything was going faster than any of the students had ever experienced before. Classes flew by, meals were inhaled, and suddenly everyone was backstage all dressed up, in full make up, ready to go. So much hubbub was happening that Thursday night was limited to only families of the students. The public could come and watch Friday or Saturday night. All the kids had their parents blessing to go to the local diner Saturday night after striking the set.

Roman peeked an eye out of the curtain. The lights over the audience hadn't gone out yet. He saw his mom and Angelica sitting next together, with their husbands on their other sides. Roman saw his grandparents and some aunts and uncles. "Aw geeze," he thought, "They could've just stayed home to watch online." Most of the seats were filled and Roman saw a couple arguing with each other and causing a commotion with one of the ushers. They were sat in the very back and seemed angry they didn't get preferential seating. "Well, that's what you get for not being on time." Roman mused.

Suddenly the lights over the audience dimmed and a spotlight hit Mr. Henderson as he walked towards a microphone as the audience clapped.

"Family and friends of our student performers! Welcome and greetings to all of you and happy performance day. Our students have been working tirelessly to bring this old story made new again to life. None of this would be possible without their dedication and passion. I am so honored to have been able to work with two graduate students from our local university."

Mr. Henderson brought up Brendan and Candice, thanked all the parents that volunteered, and any of the local businesses that sponsored the production. Roman was suddenly jerked back by the shoulders.

"Hey there, Romeo, don't go spoiling the show before it starts. Get in your character's head man, c'mon, c'mon!" It was J hassling him and shuffling him out of the way of the curtain crew. "Go break a leg, Romeo!"

"Wrong play, J. You better watch it, don't mention the Scottish Play or somebody might just break a leg." Roman glanced around with faux fright.

"Oooh baby is somebody superstitious, I never took you for the type!" J batted her eyelashes up at Roman who actually grinned and reached over for his character's cape and sword.

"Not superstitious, but still, it's better not to rattle Fate's cage. She is a fickle one. Good luck to yourself, I'm loving the soundtrack. We've got to talk to Candice and Brendan about making a YouTube channel to load up the music and the play so it gets more recognition."

"For sure." J looked like she was about to say more, but was cut off by the students playing Giacomo, Antonio, and Puccino saying the prologue together. That was Roman's cue and J slipped back to the shadows.

"A Tuesday came in December, where the day was as short as night is in June, full of auspicious happiness. This day of Mars, red and burning, is the day of a Slavic princess and the story of her finding someone worthy of her love and care. For while her spirit burned bright with rage, she could turn her heart to cruel and cold ice. We present this story to you for your enjoyment and wonder." The three students introduced the play and bowed to polite applause. They slipped off stage as Roman took the stage and began the play.

Everything was bold and smooth. Going beat by beat. Scene two started and Roman gave Rose knuckles as she took her spot on stage on some risers meant to look like a tower looking down on the path Roman's character was taking up. The audience laughed as Roman snuck behind Bethany and some other students pretended to "die" and fall apart as some of the guardians of the castle. Sloane worked a stage fan to blow an airplane Rose tried to throw down as a warning. If the audience had been wowed by Roman's introduction, they were mesmerized by Rose's performance. There was one short pause at the beginning of the third scene when there was an interruption towards the back of the theater where Roman had seen the arguing couple, but Rose regained her composure and began talking harshly towards Roman that was so uncharacteristic of her. Pillars of tissue paper fire rustled on either side of her and wearing heels and a few steps above Roman on the risers she was truly an awe inspiring, intimidating, beauty. Her make up made her seem so highly esteemed and mature. Not a force that anyone would take lightly. Roman and Rose bantered back and forth flawlessly. Act I came to a close and Rose needed to switch make-up and costumes, but grabbed Roman and J.

"I think my parents are here!" Rose felt panic that she hadn't shown on stage.

"What the hell, really? How fucking dare they! Well, my dad is here, Roman's dad is here, there is no way they will be able to try shit here." J was starting to shake with anger.

"Are they uh, kind of an older Vietnamese couple? The man wearing a blue button up shirt and slacks and balding and uh the lady kind of looks like J's dad but with longer hair and really short?

I saw a couple come in late and argue with the ushers." Roman kind of stumbled over trying to describe them since even with glasses his distance vision wasn't the best.

J and Rose stared at him and started laughing, nearly unable to control themselves. That broke the mood, especially when J said sarcastically, "Yes Roman, Rose's parents are Vietnamese, if you haven't noticed we both are."

"That does sound like them. I can't believe they're actually here. J can you message your dad? I'm going to pretend they aren't here."

Rose went to get changed, J helped switch the music and setting, and Roman got ready for his longer scene with Bethany as the Watchman. Act II Scene 1 is all Roman and Bethany discussing morality while "burying" the decapitated heads that had been on the wall of the fortress. This gave Rose all the time she needed for a costume change.

24 Juliet

J went to help Rose as soon as the set was struck for the different act. Rose was fine, almost eerily confident and poised. J wanted to fight someone, but Rose calmed her down.

"No sense in ruining the show, that would let them win. Besides, it might not even be them." Rose said while getting false eyelashes and sequins placed around her eyes.

"I know, but I'm going to give Mr. Henderson a heads up and have him let me text my dad. I think this counts as an emergency." J explained and Rose nodded ever so slightly to give her blessing.

"They probably saw the paper. Saw my picture, me and Roman, I mean they are my parents. I didn't think they'd have any interest in coming. They probably wouldn't have if slimy Tyler hadn't gotten in trouble. They only remember I exist when they want someone to do something for him." Rose actually sat up taller and more confident as her face was finished. Act II Scene 1 ended with Roman coming off the stage and getting some water and freshening up his stage makeup. J went and talked with Mr. Henderson who let her have her phone to message her dad and take it back. Act II Scene 2 was the three students playing the court servants and the executioner talking. The kid playing the executioner was a freshman, but he was huge for his age. He was a wrestler and football player and was an absolute ham, bounding around stage teasing the other actors and flaunting a toy axe. The crowd roared with laughter as his small part stole the show. The children had also really loved his part!

Scene 3 had Roman's prince getting acquainted with the servants and closed out the second act. J was busy rearranging the set and helping Sloane with different props. The main draw of the first scene of Act III was Prince Bjorn and Nasrin-Nush playing Nine Men's Morris. The fancy board was set up with a teacher's document camera looking down at the board while it was displayed on three screens at the back and sides of the stage so the audience could see how it was played. Roman actually had pushed for the rules and game play to be added to a page of the program. Very few of the parents hadn't already learned about it from their children, though.

This part of the play was probably the most difficult for them to get the pacing right. Remembering how to play the game the same each time and get their lines and inflection correct was a challenge that Roman loved and Rose had despised. Still they persevered and gave an astounding performance. Especially the part where Rose's character gets to throw a fit at Roman and scream. For someone who had always been quiet and a wall flower it was a joy to see her fall into the rageful princess role.

Scene 2 of Act III had Nasrin-Nush's father, King Mikhail, join the play finally. This was the one part that Sloane had got understudy for, but had decided to switch out for Friday or Saturday with the lead. A long table had been placed out and the court servants and Bethany's Watchman character shuffled back and forth across the table while Rose, Roman, and the kid playing the king all pretended to eat and banter. The challenges of the princess continued with her testing the prince's ability to gauge symbolism and jewelry. Rose was delighted to get to use a scale from the math department and a mortar and pestle from the science department. Getting to tell her pretend father off was delightful and she hoped against hope her parents were in the audience. The anger and frustration bubbled up through her into her role. Never in her house could she have ever gotten away with being dismissive, rude, or haughty. Playing a role so different to her experience was the ultimate liberation.

Scene II ended and Roman and Rose had to quickly switch into wedding costumes as did some other characters, though for them this was just a change in head wear or cloak. Sloane and J's team moved the table back and brought out rows of chairs. The Executioner character got to be the "flower girl" and his dramatic skip prancing delighted the audience. The end of the play wrapped up with a much happier ending than the opera. The three students playing the servants came out and gave the epilogue as they had given the opening prologue.

"We hope you enjoyed this modern take on an ancient tale. Nasrin-Nush and Bjorn ruled for many and a happy year with their joyful kingdom prosperous and mighty. They also enjoyed learning and teaching each other. And yes, eventually Bjorn told Nasrin-Nush the secrets of the way to end every game of Mills in a draw."

The actors and backstage crew all came out to a standing ovation and they bowed and waved joyfully. Mr. Henderson gave a final thank you and dismissed the families to the parking lot, but did so in a way that most left without having to see Rose's parents. Mercutio had snuck backstage during the end and picked Roman up and was trying to run back and forth with him. The cast was trying to get changed back into regular clothes and get everything set up for tomorrow's performance. It was still a school night after all.

Sloane locked arms with J who locked arms with Rose who locked arms with Roman who locked arms with Mercutio. Bethany was on the other side of the theater chatting with her parents and the parents of the girl that had played Kari, the prince's servant. Most everyone else had left fairly quickly and the parking lot was pretty empty. The five students had to go sideways to get outside the door without unlinking their arms. That's when they saw a few police squad cars off to the side and their parents standing around talking with officers.

"Absolutely unacceptable for a young woman to behave in such a way! Your daughter and your wild ways have corrupted our little girl! You should be ashamed of yourselves! You stole our daughter!" Rose's dad was being put in a police car and her mom was arguing with police officers.

The five kids froze at this and thank goodness the car drove away before Rose's dad saw her. Charles and Angelica walked over quickly with Roman's parents and Mercutio's mom following behind. There was no way Rose's mom would confront that many adults without her husband backing her up. She was fuming and stormed off to her car.

"I actually had the order of protection on me. I guess they thought if they showed up in person they could bully us into talking to them and force you to go home with them." Charles said as he hugged his niece and daughter. "That was amazing, all of you!" He shook the boys' hands vigorously.

The kids all muttered their thanks and appreciation and Valerie revealed that she had gotten bouquets for Rose and J. Rose started to cry out of pure happiness and feeling so lucky to find safe adults that appreciated her for herself. Then a round of hugging began and shortly everyone shuffled into their own cars and went on to their own homes. More often than not family is who shows up for you and builds you up, not the one that fate might have dealt to a person at first.

173

25 Romeo

Friday and Saturday's performances were much less eventful with the audience. They mixed up the roles and it was a lot more fun to take turns and share parts with the entire class. A group of such different kids wound up getting fairly close. Mr. Henderson, Brendan, and Candice wound up joining everyone at the local 24 hour diner for a little bit after they finished tearing down. Roman was even able to talk a few kids into playing Mills with him. Sloane's mom showed up and drove Roman, J, and Rose home.

Without the play and without anything to cram for studying, Roman had a rare experience of boredom. He read, played volleyball, but such a sudden and drastic change in schedule wore on him. He liked being busy and he liked his routine. Suddenly having quiet time again was jarring. The experience with the play had helped him decide one thing: what to do after high school.

Roman was a shoe-in for valedictorian. He wrote his speech effortlessly and went through all the senior year celebrations. To his surprise his mom had mellowed out a lot. He had been sure the sooner it got to his graduation the worse her nagging and empty nester feeling would start to take over. Instead his parents were planning on doing a little traveling here and there to stay busy. Watching her plan was like watching a college kid get ready to go on spring break for the first time. Good thing his dad knew how to keep her out of trouble. Once a party girl, always a party girl, Roman mused.

J's family came to graduation since Rose was also graduating. Mercutio almost got stuck in summer school, but got the last few credits by the skin of his teeth. Rose was staying in town to take courses in public health and help pioneer drug treatment and addiction recovery. Mercutio was going to just start doing pre-reqs at the community college and work part time at Roman's family's restaurant. From their seats on the field Roman could see Sloane and J sitting together and resting their heads on top of each others. Mr. Henderson was one of the teachers on stage helping with diplomas. Principal Andrews introduced all of the speakers and seemed even prouder than usual for the students of Verona High. Finally it was time for speeches and Roman went up to speak.

"Good evening to everyone here tonight in our school community! It has been a long and short four years of high school. I have learned and grown so much even just this last year as a senior. If someone had told me in eighth grade that I would do everything I have accomplished, I would have called them a liar. If anyone told me this time last year that I would have taken drama and actually enjoyed it I would have bet them my next few years in secondary school over how wrong you were. Good thing nobody tried that, or else I'd have no say in what I've decided to do with my next chapter in life.

The most important thing that high school has taught me is the value of friends and community. None of us can do everything alone. We need each other. We need family. Friends. Teachers. Counselors. Role models. We are role models for younger children, and that can be a huge thing to realize. Our time here is to learn about the past and apply these lessons to brighten our future. Community and cooperation are vital to the continuation of our society. We must not lose sight of that. One thing I hope you take away from me tonight is the idea that you are part of our greater community. How can we forge forward to build a safe and loving community? Every small thing you choose, even the tiniest of actions, has an impact on everything around you with ripple effects.

I know I've wrestled at length about what I should do. I'm barely eighteen. How on earth does that make me an adult? The choices I make impact the rest of my future. So many paths I could take and I have the privilege that many do not - to have choice. I did work very hard to be where I am now and my future has always been important to me. With great excitement I get to tell everyone what I've been keeping secret for weeks. I've been accepted to Cornell University on a full ride! I will be majoring in law with a focus on public defense and minoring in acting! Thank you all for being there for me and believing in me. This town, this school, the teachers and coaches, and my parents and family have all empowered me and I need to spend the rest of my life returning the favor and great faith you all have trusted in me. I humbly hope I am up to the challenge and can support others as much as you have all supported me. Thank you."

The crowd stood and applauded Roman as he returned to his spot and all his buddies close by shook him and gave him shoulder punches. The seniors all filed up to get their diplomas and the ceremony commenced. The families all went out to dinner and went over to Roman's house afterwards to talk and play video games.

Roman was sitting outside in his backyard on a step watching the stars and J came out to sit by him, smoothing her skirt under her as she lowered down next to him and looked up.

"So you'll be leaving at the end of July?"

"Mhm that's the plan. Get settled in up in the dorm and find my way around."

"Going to try and learn how to drive before you leave? I think my mom and Rose could help if you want."

"Nah, I've got a bike and Ithica has a really good public transportation system."

"You sure? You might change your mind when the snow starts piling up."

"We'll see. Maybe when you learn how to drive you can give me lessons."

They smiled at each other and looked back up to the stars.

"Roman, I really am glad you were here at school with me this year. Next year is going to be strange without you. I'll miss you."

"Aw, you'll be fine. You've made friends, you've got Sloane. You can make sure people stay in line."

"Thanks, man, can I give you a hug?"

"Sure."

They awkwardly hugged, and missed a shooting star going over the trees and past the houses. J stood up and told Roman bye. She ran inside and left with her parents. Roman stayed just for a few more breaths and got up and went in to hang out with his parents.

Epilogue

St. Peter was looking down at the two teenagers smiling. Finally, finally had their souls found peace. No longer would their families be chased with disaster and tragedy. The true way to break their curse was to find the love of themselves and the respect of each other as individuals. Romantic love is not the only love humans can share with each other.

Rose achieved her dreams and helped heal damage done by drug abuse in the community. She became a community expert and the programs she spearheaded spread across communities all over the world. Her parents divorced and through therapy she has a relationship with her mom. Tyler got out of prison and made good choices and worked to strengthen his relationship with his mom and sister. Rose talks to people that addiction is not the end of their lives and that there is more that they can fight for with Tyler's help.

Mercutio became a teacher and works at the local middle school. He and his partner got married and adopted several children. They are vocal volunteer advocates for LGBTQ programs across their county.

Julianna graduated high school and became involved in social work and works closely running programs with the public libraries in the county. She performs music out of love and charity for it. Despite her immense talent being in the limelight was never truly her desire. Hollywood and the music industry was always terribly superficial and her true punk heart would not allow her to follow that path.

Sloane stayed friends with Rose and Julianna, although they did not continue dating after high school. Junior year he discovered a passion for working with cars and became a mechanic. He works around town helping to keep families in lower income brackets keep their vehicles. Eventually he worked with the city to find new ways to design roads to be more pedestrian friendly in their urban planning development.

Roman graduated college with full honors. He did a few small acting roles in TV shows and movies, but used this more to raise awareness about injustices in the legal system. Acting really did help him in his legal career to pace out situations and get inside of others' heads to see people's ulterior motives. Through hard work and dedication he eventually became the first Cuban American Supreme Court Justice.

People are more the same than they are different. Most people try to do the best they can, there are few people truly out in the world actively trying to cause more strife and suffering. All people struggle and have hardship. The goal is to remember to strive for good despite how difficult life gets. If everyone could learn how to put others first and practice radical empathy then more pains and hurts could be reconciled.

Nasrin-Nush

Cast of Characters:

Princess Nasrin-Nush——————————-—A Slavic Princess Determined to Stay Unwed Rose

King Mikhail ———————————————Father of Nasrin-Nush Sloane as Understudy

Giacomo————————————————————Servant of the Royal Family

ETERNALLY STAR-CROSSED HATERS

Antonio———————————————————Servant of the Royal Family

Puccinio——————————————————Servant of the Royal Family

Executioner——————————————Beheads Those Who Fail the Riddle Challenge

Watchman—————————————————Guards the Castle Bethany

King Harold————————————————Deposed King of a Nordic Country in Exile

Prince Bjorn—————————————————Son of King Harold Roman

Kari————————————————————Servant of King Harold

Common People———————————————The Citizens of Princess Nasrin-Nush

Act I

<u>Prologue</u>

"A Tuesday came in December, where the day was as short as night is in June, full of auspicious happiness. This day of Mars, red and burning, is the day of a Slavic princess and the story of her finding someone worthy of her love and care. For while her spirit burned bright with rage, she could turn her heart to cruel and cold ice. We present this story to you for your enjoyment and wonder."

Scene 1

Scene: Prince Bjorn studies the painting of Princess Nasrin-Nush at the gate of the palace. Severed heads line the fence all around the fortress. An older man and young woman approach him.

KARI

181 "

"Bjorn? Prince Bjorn? It is! It's you!" *[Kari cries and leads the older man to embrace the prince.]*

BJORN

"Father? Kari? Well by what divine intervention have I found you both?" *[Prince Bjorn returns the embraces, but steps back all of a sudden.]*

KING HAROLD

"What is the matter my son?" *[King Harold is blind and confused at his son's distance.]*

BJORN

"I am here at this fortress's first gate to take on the challenge that has been plaguing the land. I arrived in this metropolis after we lost our country to rebellion and treachery. I have watched as other young princes like myself took the challenge and were killed over and over again."

KING HAROLD

"My son, what is this you speak of? Kari and I have wandered for these many months alone in an unloving land." *[The three move to the gates where there is a wood engraving of a woman's face. Kari moves the king's hands so he can feel the image.]*

BJORN

"There is a princess in this kingdom, beautiful and fiery as she is cold and wicked. She has decreed that none may have her hand in marriage if they cannot solve the challenges she has laid forth in this fortress. Failure is death. I admit that I, too, fell in love at first sight of her image, but this is above all else a moral outrage that so many lives have been lost so senselessly. So here I wait, ready to attempt my luck at the tests before me."

KARI

"My prince, you cannot! The walls around the entire city are spiked with the heads of the wretched who have tried, it is not possible, please rethink this."

BJORN

"Ah, Kari, so sweet. I know it looks dire, but on my side I have the benefit of the education my father provided for me, the experience of the travels I have endured, and the calm patience to plan my actions."

[The gate slowly opens and the emissary of the princess exits the path from the fortress heading towards the center of the city]

BJORN

"Notice, there, the trusted guard of the princess. Once a week they come into the city to visit the king in his palace and to return with supplies. They are not bothered by the stone guardians that maim any other who attempts to travel that perilous road. I will wait for them to return this evening and follow in behind, wearing this." *[The prince unfurls a red cloak complete with a hood]*

BJORN

"This princess loves crimson as is evidenced by the blood that has been spilt by the never tiring guardians up the narrow path to her palace. If only I can get past that I am further than any of these other poor souls have gotten and that much closer to ending this madness. I have learned that the spell may be broken when one clothed in red passes a guardian, the Watchman wears blue and black, I shall be victorious in red. This will fulfill the first condition of the challenge listed on the notice by the portrait of this wretched princess."

KING HAROLD

"My son, I have only just been reunited with you and it is your plan to now leave us just as soon? You say that is only the first condition? What other torments are you going to have to face?"

KARI

"My king, the first challenge is true, to safely travel the path to the fortress and destroy those enchanted guardians. The second challenge is finding the door into the fortress itself. The walls are smooth and solid with no great gate or draw bridge. It is pure sorcery that this brazen fort stands in the harsh light. And the impossible door must be found, it wouldn't count to come in from the sky. If our prince can finish these feats of strength he must follow the princess back to her father's home and await three more tasks in order to keep his life and earn this wicked woman's hand in marriage."

PRINCE HAROLD

"My son, this is an insurmountable challenge. Let us leave and create a happy, peaceful, and simple life together. I do not want to lose you as I have lost my kingdom and fortune."

BJORN

"Father, I leave you to do right by the world and you have done well these past few years. Kari has done well to love and care for you in my stead and forever I am thankful." *[Bjorn turns to Kari and touches their cheek as they swoon and shakes themself back into their duty]*

KARI

"Please heed our concern, my dear prince! I would rather die a thousand deaths than allow any harm to come to you. Your father and I do not doubt your resourcefulness and brave heart, but we worry you will suffer the same fate as these other pitiful suitors. Who would want to join themselves to a woman so certain to be left in solitude? Do not kick the hornet's nest, this is a test set up only for failure, though I do not doubt you can be successful in getting past the first step."

BJORN

"Then let my sacrifice, if indeed it is destined to be such, serve as the final example to all that the Lady of the Castle Keep does want nothing more than to be lonely for her days. For if I cannot conquer the challenges the most ingenious maiden has set up, let it be known that no one will be able to. Come, let us retire and spend the day together before returning for my task this evening."

Scene 2

Scene: The set pulls back and moves up to the top of the fortress as the princess looks down at the gate from a telescope on her balcony. She pulls her hair back as she paces and lets it slowly fall from her fingers.

NASRIN-NUSH

"So it seems that man has finally left the gate after so many weeks. Humph. I am glad for it, it has begun to bore me whether he will or will not attempt the trek up to the fortress. Not that if he were to survive he would understand how to get into the castle. When will these men realize it is useless to come and try to subjugate me? I am the most beautiful, true, or so they tell me, but I have still not met the man or woman who is my equal in that of my knowledge and studies. I will not marry, I will not lessen myself to one who is not worthy of my mind and heart. There is no happiness in that."

[Lightening gradually changes from white to red to signify time passing and the sun setting. The princess is on a raised set of risers and pours herself a drink, reads a book, and plays a board game against herself]

NASRIN-NUSH

"The Watchman should be returning now. Let's see what is going on in the city below." *[as the princess rises to look through her telescope she sees her Watchman entering the gate, but the stranger has returned without his companions. He is too far behind for the Watchman to notice, yet close enough to observe the specific way the Watchman avoids the stone and iron guardians. Carefully timing himself to avoid the steady and chopping bidents. The stranger copies the Watchman in a limbo/hopscotch like obstacle course wearing the red cloak that makes it hard to see him in the red setting sun. Each time the stranger passes a guardian, they collapse and fall apart.]*

NASRIN-NUSH

"IMPOSSIBLE! NO! No, no, no, no, no! How can this be, oh there is no time to get a warning to my Watchman!" *[Here she scurries to her desk to scribble on a paper, fold it into an airplane, and throw it below. A fan blows it straight back into the room.]*

NASRIN-NUSH

"WATCHMAN! LOOK OUT! BEHIND YOU NOTICE THE KNAVE STALKING BEHIND YOU! Oh it is no use! I've built the fortress too tall and the wind is too strong for my cries to be heard." *[The princess paces before returning to her telescope to peer down at their progress]* "No matter. He can follow the Watchman to the wall. There is no door. He will be helpless to enter and will either starve at the foot of my brazen fort or be slaughtered when he turns to retreat in defeat. It is fine."

[The Watchman and the prince have reached the wall of the fortress by this point. As they both passed a guardian the spell that had been placed on them fell apart and they were ruined. The princess notices this and stomps her foot as the Watchman returns back to her chamber.]

WATCHMAN

"I have returned, Your Highness, and I have brought a present from your father. He has sent candied dates and nuts for you to enjoy. I hope you were comfortable in my absence." *[The princess roughly takes the bag and sets it on her desk and paces to the telescope and gestures for the Watchman to peer down at the base of the fortress. Seeing the prince having set up a camp at the wall with a fire they step back, arms wide, and collapse to the floor bowing deeply.]*

WATCHMAN

"My most esteemed lady, I do not deserve to serve you. I did not notice this interloper and have failed in my duty to protect you and your heart. I accept my punishment fully and immediately."

NASRIN-NUSH

[The princess roughly grabs the Watchman up by their arm.] "That's enough, you fool! You have not failed your duty to me, and I still value your service. I am just astounded that there is a man alive clever enough to figure out how to avoid you, the steady slice of the guardians, and to know that by wearing all red the spell would be ruined. Let us watch and see what he does next. There is no way to get in, I watched and he missed the trick to get in, although he does know the area about where you vanished from his view." *[She hands a smaller telescope to them and they peer down at the prince.]*

BJORN

"Hopefully I will not need to stay here for too long. I had to stay far enough behind to not be discovered, but in the failing light could not see where or how the emissary gained entry to the fortress. The walls are solid. Iron. I have never seen such precise engineering in all of my learning or travels." *[Bjorn touches the walls and stalks back and forth, whistling steadily. The lighting gradually changes from red, to dark with just the glow of his campfire, to the rise of a silver blue moon.]*

BJORN

"Metal has different frequencies. When tapped, like responds with like. While constructed to look like one solid piece the seam of the portal must be too small for the eye to see or hand to feel. There must be a way to find it." *[The prince gets a torch and turns back down the path as the princess and the Watchman peer anxiously down.]* "Ah-hah! Of course. I'd say it is so simple, but of course it isn't. Each of these guardians had an identical bident, unlike any weapon ever before seen. Twin blades set into just one hilt. Not very effective for war, but something so beautiful and unique cannot just have one sole purpose. No. Not for such a cunning and clever person as the princess."

NASRIN-NUSH

"Wait. No, what is he doing? I thought he had already given up, but he's gone back for one of the swords!" *[The princess grabs at the Watchman and grabs their small tuning fork key that allowed them entry into and out of the fortress's hidden gate.]* I trust your loyalty and silence more than I trust myself my friend, but how on earth has this simple man put the pieces together so quickly? My father doesn't even know the answers to my secrets that I have constructed!"

WATCHMAN

"I fear this man may not be mortal! Shall I prepare to try and slit his throat and free his head from his shoulders if he does gain entry?"

NASRIN-NUSH

"No, of course not, no. I have set up a terrible challenge, but I will not be a deceitful murderer. The conditions of the challenge will not change. Even if he gains entry and we return to my father's home he has three more puzzles to solve. Whether he be man or immortal is irrelevant to us right now. If the gods have decided to solve my challenge to humble me I will have to face my fate with dignity and grace."

WATCHMAN

"Of course my lady." *[The Watchman squeezes the princess's shoulder reassuringly.]*

BJORN

"My music teacher taught me how to tune my lyre as a boy using a special fork. Tap and feel the energy of music. The first challenge was of physical skill, this is a challenge of music and physics."

[Bjorn uses his dagger to tap the much larger two-pronged bident and places it to the wall over and over while talking.]

"In sword fighting it isn't just skill or strength that determine who wins a fight. With each swing and strike, the vibrations move through your blade and wane the strength from your very muscles. Stamina is the greatest ability a swordsman needs in this world."

[After several strikes the door to the palace shudders in response and slides open to allow Bjorn to enter.]

BJORN

"May the gods be with me as I continue my quest and I give thanks to have made it so far with my head still intact."

NASRIN-NUSH

"You know what my dear friend?"

WATCHMAN

"Yes, Your Highness?"

NASRIN-NUSH

"I'm starting to think that maybe it's about time that somebody figures my riddles out. Come, I will prepare to meet this wily suitor in my throne room. Bring him to me."

Scene 3

Scene: Princess Nasrin-Nush sits in a tall throne with pillars of fire on either side, dressed in a long red gown, red lipstick, red eyeshadow, and a tall and severe expression. The Watchman leads Prince Bjorn in to see her.

NASRIN-NUSH

"Welcome to you, one who is skilled in the ways of solving challenges of physical prowess, fortune and good luck favors you to bring you into my fortress where countless before you have failed. You must surely know that I am Princess Nasrin-Nush and what I will require further of you. While you are sweet to look upon, I am more pleased that you were able to use knowledge to get so far. I wonder, why are you not already married, at home with your wife. Are you cruel or unkind to have been unable to find a partner as of yet?"

BJORN

"My fairest of ladies. It is my honor to have arrived at the foot of your throne. I will leave it up to you to decide whether I be cruel or unkind, but that is fairly humorous coming from one who has caused so much slaughter of young lives."

NASRIN-NUSH

"Slaughter? Caused by my hand? I believe you forget every man who has taken up this challenge had the full choice to turn away and I have simply been sitting here living my own life as I please. Filling my days creating art, researching the condition of existence, and thinking deeply of the questions of philosophy. Living in my father's palace I could not get a moment's peace to do as I desired with my time. Princes interrupting me, telling me what a woman's place should be. I know my place and it is not to be beholden to some man who thinks I should make myself small for their comfort because of my beauty and my status in this life. So tell me, does the desire to be uninterrupted or forced into marriage make me cruel and unkind?"

BJORN

"I must admit that now that I hear your full reasoning for this extravagance from you that I understand your plight."

NASRIN-NUSH

"Hah. I am sure you understand *nothing* of me in just one introduction. I question the motives of any man who is motivated by simply knowing I am the crown princess and thus heir of my father's rich country and am beautiful. What is your motivation for this journey?"

BJORN

"Justice."

NASRIN-NUSH

"Excuse me?"

BJORN

"If you forgive me, my lady, but it is not just that so many souls have been lost in the pursuit of your most elegant hand. I do admit I was moved in my heart by the image of your beauty carved on the gate to your fortress, but I did not desire to be your husband for my own gain, but only to save any other man who may wind up in my position."

NASRIN-NUSH

"That may be more surprising than what I could have ever expected. I am still suspicious of you. The first condition is that you must be of a royal birth, so if you do get past this point, I do hope you are ready to show that you are worthy of one such as me in all respects. It would be a pity to lose someone who has gotten so far and seems at first appearance to be noble. Sleep now, my Watchman will come for you and bring you to my father's home where we will continue the challenges in two days."

[The Watchman leads the prince away while the princess watches and is lost in deep thought. The Watchman returns and kneels before the princess.]

NASRIN-NUSH

"I do believe we must begin our journey back to my father's palace. It is still dark and we can enter undisturbed. I'm sure that few in the city have realized that the first two challenges have been defeated. You have a long journey ahead of you. Already to town and back once, I must thank you for serving me for so long so faithfully my friend."

[The princess rises from her throne as it fades into the background and the two begin to leave the fortress and walk down the path past the fallen guardians and into the city as they talk.]

WATCHMAN

"It is my purpose to serve you, Your Highness, I could walk back and forth a thousand times without rest for you. I do worry about what happens next for you. I do not want to see you coupled against your will if it truly is to be alone."

NASRIN-NUSH

"In the beginning it was, but it has been many years now, and I know my father will need me to step up as a strong ruler. And if I have to marry, I would never be content with anyone who could not match me as an equal."

WATCHMAN

"What happens in the event that he cannot solve the next puzzles? Do we set the guardians up again? Reseal the wall? Create new challenges?"

[By this point they are at the entry to the city palace]

NASRIN-NUSH

"I think... we will worry about that when it needs to be worried about. It might be time to work on a new angle. For now, return to the fortress, take a rest, and return with our new challenger in two days. I must go see my father."

[The princess kisses the Watchman on the cheek as she goes off stage to enter the palace and the Watchman walks back to the fortress as the sun rises.]

BJORN

"Ah, there you are my friend, I hope this morning light is finding you well."

WATCHMAN

"Well enough in this new chapter of my life. We have been alone in this fortress for many years. It doesn't quite feel real that someone has been successful in the challenges. I thank you for your bravery, but you must fully know that if I had been aware of your trickery I would have been required to end you."

BJORN

"Fully understood and I must apologize for the subterfuge, I had been worried that if you failed in your duties you may have suffered as similarly as those whose heads decorate the walls of the city."

WATCHMAN

"I also considered that I would suffer a similar fate. Our Princess, however, is not as cold and cruel as would be believed. She is wise and just desires to be seen for more than only her beauty. I do not believe another woman of her prestige has ever graced this world."

BJORN

"I think... She is just not afraid to demand what she desires, now that I have met her face to face. It is true that her physical beauty is overwhelming, to the point of causing one to lose their own common sense. Most women want love, though, for who they are in their hearts and minds."

WATCHMAN

"Sir, I am glad that it is you who has begun to break this challenge and bring peace to the princess of our country. I must rest, but you are free to eat in the kitchen, read in the library, and walk in the gardens at your leisure. I will see you at meals and tomorrow evening we will head to the palace. I must warn you that already the city is rejoicing at the news that someone has gotten as far as you have. We will have a lot of attention and little peace. You're not home free yet, and if you're not ready for the challenges of the mind your head will still be up on one of those pikes. This time I may actually cry for you."

[Patting the prince heartily on the back the Watchman retires to their quarters leaving the prince to think deeply on what will come next]

Act II

Scene 1

[The Watchman appears to see the prince out at the city walls with a shovel]

WATCHMAN

"Ah, there you are sir, I was worried you had left out of fear of the next tests and we would have to send assassins after you for abandoning your quest half way!"

BJORN

"Abandon? No, no, nothing of the sort."

[The prince continues to dig while talking]

WATCHMAN

"So, ah, what are you working on, exactly? You could be resting and enjoying the luxuries of the fortress today and the next before continuing on to the last challenges. Maybe reading some of the books our fair lady has left behind may give you some insight over the next trial?"

BJORN

"While that would indeed be useful, that serves only me. For now I cannot rest until I lay these challengers that came before me to rest."

[The prince climbs up the wall to secure a few of the heads on pikes and returns down to bury them]

BJORN

"Since I have begun this story's end I am giving these unfortunate princes a burial so they may find some peace in the afterlife that they were cheated out of here on Earth."

WATCHMAN

"No one forced them to take up the challenge. Better it be for them to heed such warnings and leave well enough alone if they had any sense."

BJORN

"Oh really? It's so easy to just 'have sense' as a prince? Have the pressures and expectations of making your father, your homeland, proud? Ignore the challenge of a century and be defeated by a woman? That's how most of these lads thought I am sure. Instead of giving a suitor or sampling of suitors a chance that scornful princess had to set up a challenge no man could pass up. And I swear that door with her visage was enchanted. A mere wood carving that made her hair look like a blanket of the night sky that would wrap up any who love her. Eyes that burn with the deepest wisdom and passion. Full, sumptuous lips that one could just lean forward and kiss..."

[The prince pauses in his work and leans forward as if to kiss the door.]

WATCHMAN

"Many did."

BJORN

"What is that?"

[The prince is shaken awake from the daydream and continues to bury the heads, while kneeling and saying a silent prayer before beginning a new grave.]

WATCHMAN

"Many kissed the engraving she made. We were always watching the gate, you know, keeping tabs on the city and any who may accept the challenge. I'm surprised the lips were not worn off of the door from which it is carved."

BJORN

"Again, I would have chalked it up to an enchantment. A magic spell. That there was no physical way a woman could ever possibly be half as beautiful as that carving. But now, now I have seen our princess and yesterday I would not have believed anyone who told me that the carving didn't do her justice. I guess now I can half understand the reason for this ridiculous loss of life. What lengths one must feel compelled to go just so that they know someone is not just with them for what they gain in a wife."

[The prince retrieves more heads from the wall while talking and stares into the decaying face in his hands before burying another]

WATCHMAN

"All of us on Earth. Young or old, man or woman, rich or poor; we all truly want to find that love and that connection with each other. To trust and rely on the ones in our immediate circle to be there to support and guide us through life. Here, I will help you with the task of laying the dead to rest. Together we shall do this and talk and learn from each other. I did not have the chance to know any of these other challengers, but nevertheless I am glad that you are the one to have made it this far in this endeavor."

BJORN

"And if I have come this far to only fail what next awaits me I will be glad to have known you and have your help in my task for the next few days. I thank you my friend, let us get busy and not let these gruesome adornments haunt this city any longer."

Scene 2

[Scene: The citizens have gathered out on the streets surrounding the palace having a huge party. In the vestibule the servants prepare for the upcoming trials.]

GIACOMO

"Tell us again what the Watchman said before they returned back up to the fortress?"

ANTONIO

"He arrived in the dead of night with the princess hidden in a cloak. She went to see her father and then to her chambers to prepare. The Watchman returned up to the fortress to bring the newest challenger down tomorrow!"

PUCCINIO

"And the prince! He is a prince, correct? What is this prince's name? What kingdom does he hail from?"

GIACOMO

"Yes, yes! We must announce something about this mysterious man to the people, to our king! How can we say some stranger has materialized from nothing!"

ANTONIO

"According to the Watchman he was handsome, brave, and clever beyond imagining. A name he did not provide. Nothing about his person betrayed his original origin. He survived the guardians and figured out the secret of the fortress wall. I'm still not sure what we should prepare for next. I'm not sure what we should tell the throng amassed outside the palace. I don't think any thought this day would truly come! For a man to make it this far after so many have failed, I fear how the people may react if he still meets the fate of others."

[A cloaked figure steps out of the shadows and speaks to the three servants.]

EXECUTIONER

"As far as my axe is concerned we look forward to the chance to do our job and not leave the killing to the witchcraft the princess dabbles in. Hopefully this man succeeds and turns the princess into a proper woman or if he fails I get to add a handsome head to the others on the wall."

PUCCINIO

"A head you may gain, yes, but look out across the way to the wall of the fortress and see what has been happening."

[The servants and executioner with his axe climb up the stairs above the palace gates. In the distance they can see the princess's fortress, and the absence of heads adorning its walls. They peer from the side of the balcony so the crowd below doesn't see them.]

PUCCINIO

"I wonder who it is that has started to put those other challengers to rest and how our princess will feel about it when she sees what has been done to her legacy."

EXECUTIONER

"Blast! I am torn. I admit I was jealous to not be the one to cause such death, but now to see all of that gruesome warning removed. It's almost enough to make me cry."

ANTONIO

"You are truly a depraved and violent individual. I hope this man succeeds, as long as he is a just and good man. The world needs more hope and beauty. Not more sorrow and destruction."

EXECUTIONER

[Stretches and yawns twirling his axe over his head]

"That sounds dreadfully boring. If I cannot execute this newest challenger I hope the crowd goes into a riotous frenzy! Now that would be some excitement after such a long time of quiet and peace. Here, I'll address the crowd if you are all at a loss for words, I'm sure I will have some great nuggets of wisdom to part onto them..."

[Executioner moves to reveal himself to the crowd.]

ANTONIO and PUCCINIO

[Together they grab the arms of the Executioner and hold him back]

"Oh no, no, no that will not be necessary!"

GIACOMO

"Thank you friends. I will address the crowd to placate them and we will go and see to the continued preparations of the celebratory party. And we will all hope for a happy ending and conclusion to this entire ordeal."

[Giacomo turns to face the crowd that has amassed with a friendly smile and raises out his arms.]

"Greetings to all mild and joyous citizens of our great kingdom!"

[The crowd cheers and shouts before completely quieting down.]

"As you may well have found out that there is a new challenger to the puzzles our princess has set up and he has solved two puzzles!"

[The crowd begins to shout and get restless and Giacomo has to wave his hands to get their attention back before continuing.]

"The king has sent us to declare a holiday for the next few days. We in the palace will be closed while we complete the next stage of the challenge. There are still puzzles. There are still riddles. The princess demands a worthy equal to be her suitor and our great kingdom deserves no less than the best I am sure you will agree!"

[There is another pause to allow the citizens to yell and cheer.]

"I am gladdened to hear you all agree with me! While we are inside preparing for the challenges you are invited to celebrate and take part in riches provided at city pavilions for the next few days. We will either end with a wedding, or another funeral, but one challenger making it this far is something worth celebrating! I am sorry to inform you that we have not received the man here at this time, and are unaware of where he is from or who he is, but I promise to inform you with more updates as they become available!

[Giacomo waves as he turns and leaves from addressing the crowd as some people disperse to find food, drink, and entertainment set up throughout the city.]

ANTONIO

"Well done, brother! Fantastic work!"

PUCCINIO

"This sets our expectations and steels the people for either scenario!"

EXECUTIONER

"I would've promised to have a public beheading with souvenirs and commemorative hats!"

ANTONIO and PUCCINIO

"No one asked you! You get out of here!"

[The Executioner walks off stage twirling his axe and laughing as the servants shoo him away.]

GIACOMO

"Bread and circuses, friends. We must remember to give the common people their bread and circuses."

Scene 3

Scene: The Watchman and the prince arrive at the palace ready to accept the next challenges set forth by the princess. They walk past a line of guards and across a bridge to the palace gates.

WATCHMAN

"Well done, I see the palace servants have done well to distract most of the citizenry. They're now more concerned with celebrating than they are out of curiosity of our mission."

BJORN

"It was still quite an ordeal to make it this far, even though we exited through your secret side gate."

WATCHMAN

"You are the one who has caused all of this excitement, friend! You have done what all had thought was impossible. Now we go to meet your beloved and her esteemed father."

BJORN

"I wouldn't go as far as to call her my beloved, but I do look forward to meeting a man who has raised and supported such a daughter. She is unlike any person I have ever met in all my life. I hope to understand her cold and clever mind to see if there is anything more than a selfish heart."

WATCHMAN

"Having grown up with her and protected her I can assure you that she has depths hidden behind her stony facade. It is that heart that she guards so fiercely."

[They finish crossing the bridge and the palace doors open and allow them inside with the three servants eager and waiting.]

GIACOMO

"Ah here at last we have he who has finally come so far! I am Giacomo, royal announcer and loyal servant to the royal family."

ANTONIO

"We are all excited and honored to meet one such as yourself. I am Antonio, royal steward and loyal servant to the royal family."

PUCCINIO

"It is indeed a pleasure to meet your grace in person and please if you have any needs or desires let me know at once. I am Puccinio the chamberlain and loyal servant to the royal family."

BJORN

"Gentlemen, it is certainly an honor for me to meet all of your acquaintances. Please, if you have needs or my service I would like to offer myself to each of you! I understand the stress and hardship that comes with keeping a country running and while the king may be the head, it is his loyal and talented servants that do the real dirty work. I am now and forever at your services. While I am in your debt for causing such an upset to your already challenging positions, I am afraid I cannot yet introduce myself or explain as to why I must continue this subterfuge."

[Bjorn bows deeply to each of the three servants as he addresses them. They are surprised by his words and as he finishes the three huddle together to discuss things in a group.]

PUCCINIO

"So be it! If that is how it needs to be, so it shall be. Come then with me to allow the princess's guard to retire and refresh and to give yourself some time to groom and prepare for the banquet."

[The others leave and the Watchman nods at Bjorn and mouths, "Good luck."]

BJORN

"A banquet? I was figuring we would get right into the next round of challenges immediately. And what should I be prepared for in this, my good sir?"

PUCCINIO

"Well now you are dirty and unkempt. In no way fit to be attending a royal banquet. The king has decided to give you one final party and a joyous night as our most esteemed guest if you wind up perishing rather than solving the remaining challenges. It is the least I can do to serve you with a hot bath and fine robes. You look as if you've dug yourself out of a grave."

EXECUTIONER

[From the side of the stage.]

"I could go ahead and get a head start on that!"

[Laughing at his head start pun holding a shovel with his axe. Giacomo and Antonio appear and drag him away again with Puccinio shooting them a dirty look. Bjorn is oblivious to this happening behind him.]

BJORN

"I have not come from my own grave, but have spent the last two days working with the Watchman digging graves for the heads that have adorned the wall of the fortress all these years. A shower and fresh clothes would be most humbly appreciated."

PUCCINIO

"You and the guard spent all this time, laying these others to rest? Why? What compels you to do such a thing?"

BJORN

"Decency and justice. All those lives wasted and thrown away is what drove me to take up this quest. I have spent too much of my life watching people suffer needlessly from their own foolish mistakes. I have been no stranger to misfortune myself. A person can live their life with honor and the best choices and still face disaster. Putting such a tempting challenge in front of so many willful young men knowing that they will fail is not something I can allow to continue to happen in good conscience."

PUCCINIO

"How I wish that you had come along before all of this had taken place. Maybe if our princess had met a man of such a similar world mindset she would not have decided to go to such extremes to stay unwed."

BJORN

"Perhaps, but at that time I had not learned and traveled to be the person I am now. We can always look back on the past and wish we could have changed things, but regret is the hobby of fools. All we can do in this life is make the best choices at the time with the knowledge and resources that have been revealed to us."

PUCCINIO

"How wise and right you are, my good sir. Please enjoy your rest. Someone will come here for you to start the banquet with us shortly."

BJORN

"Thank you, friend, I will and I look forward to seeing you later tonight."

Act III

Scene 1

[Bjorn has finished his bath and is dressed in a fine outfit of blue and white. He is reclining on a couch reading one of the books that decorate his room. A knock sounds at the door.]

BJORN

[Opens the door and is surprised to see the princess dressed in a red dress glowing in sequins and her guard behind her. She carries a bag and board.]

BJORN

"My exalted one! Please, what can I do for you?
[Bjorn awkwardly bows before the two entering his room.]

Nasrin-Nush

"Do? What you can do is entertain me while we wait. I must hide somewhere from curious servants and bothersome family members. Where better to hide than in your chambers? The entire castle has been ordered to leave you alone so you may physically and mentally prepare for my next challenges. It's in my best interest to give you no such rest and I wish to be amused. You've solved two of my puzzles so I have decided to reward you with a gift of entertaining me. Tell me. Have you ever played a game called Merelles?

[The princess walks past, not acknowledging his bow, and starts setting the game up on a cushion next to a small table and the couch

Bjorn had just been laying on reading. She picked up the book he had left on the table and nodded her approval before setting it aside.]

BJORN

"I have played it many times, in many places, your grace. The most common name I've heard for it is Mills?"

NASRIN-NUSH

"Mills? Why on earth would it be called Mills?"

BJORN

"The rows and the pieces move like that of a windmill to some people."

NASRIN-NUSH

"Huh. I suppose they do. What a wonderful observation. I envy you, you know. The choice and opportunity to have traveled and experienced the world first hand where I've only been able to look at it from afar and in books is frustrating to me. Would you like to go first or second?"

BJORN

[He hesitates, but sits down and takes his pieces.]

"I would not have been able to travel and explore if it had not been for hardship and disaster. I often wonder how different life would have been if I could have stayed where I was born and lived a more quiet and stable life. Are you sure this is proper and allowed? I'm not going to get you in trouble, here having the princess alone in my quarters? This isn't a test starting already, is it?"

NASRIN-NUSH

[She laughs heartily.]

"I promise no such subterfuge. My father and family would be thrilled if I was of a mind to do anything unseemly with a man alone. Plus my guard here will protect me from any ill you would dare try to force upon me. I'm not scared of you in the least. As far as this being a trick, no, of course not. I have worked too hard and too long on my challenges to turn to tricks at the end. I have told you I am hard, but I am fair."

BJORN

"Well then. I suppose we should get to playing. Would you like to go first or second?"

NASRIN-NUSH

[Without answering she sets her first piece down and smiles at him across the table.]

WATCHMAN

"She is going to destroy you. She's only had me as an opponent for many years now and always wants to play and learn new patterns. Her father won't even play with her anymore."

BJORN

[Answers as he places his first piece and while the princess places her second.] "Winning isn't always the most interesting part of a game or challenge, especially in one like this."

[Bjorn places his second piece.]

NASRIN-NUSH

"I know exactly what you mean."

[Places her third piece and continues to talk as Bjorn places his third.]

"In fact, I grew so tired of always winning against my dear Watchman that I figured out a way I can always lose in this game."

[She places her fourth piece.]

"I actually find that much more interesting to force someone to be playing for a loss for a win."

WATCHMAN

"And I've told you that you've spent so much time alone it's warped your perspective of what a game and puzzle should be!"

207

NASRIN-NUSH

[Watches Bjorn place his fourth piece.]

"Nonsense. Playing a game the way everyone else plays it is dull. You can play the same game hundreds of times over and have it not get interesting."

[She places her fifth piece and Bjorn follows.]

"The fun is in finding new ways to play. Make losing winning and winning losing. Father still refuses to give me a chance after all this time, I tried to go visit him first. He says he's too busy preparing for tonight, but I know the truth is that he hates losing to me. And telling him losing is the new winning just frustrated him even more."

[They both place their sixth piece.]

BJORN

"So in that case are we playing to win or playing to lose?"

[They both place their seventh pieces.]

NASRIN-NUSH

"Oh I was assuming on just playing a few regular rounds. It will be dinner soon and we must go focus on other things. I like to learn about a person by how they strategize in a game. What they sacrifice and what they protect tells a lot about a person, that is, if the other person knows what to look for."

[They both place their eighth pieces.]

BJORN

"I know exactly what you mean, but so rarely am I able to explain this to other people. I, too, have struggled to find people who are willing to try new strategies or change the conditions."

[They both place their final and ninth piece.]

"I did, however, have the honor of learning many tricks to this particular game. It's come in handy many times."

NASRIN-NUSH

"Game tricks? Coming in handy?"

[Sliding one of her pieces she captures one of the prince's chips]

"How can knowing a game and trick plays come in handy?"

BJORN

"Well, it's like you said, playing a game with someone tells you a lot about who they are as a person. Games are universal to all people, no matter where they are in the world. I think to not play makes a person less than human, even less than an animal. Even animals play throughout their lives. True death and soullessness comes from those beings who have lost the will to play, learn, and grow."

[Bjorn slides a piece to block the princess from completing a Mill.]

NASRIN-NUSH

"Very true. It's important for people to have balance between work and rest, being productive and being creative. The greatest blessing is to be able to combine productivity and creativity. Something useful and beautiful that will solve problems for people and the world."

[The princess fills in another space and blocks the prince while simultaneously completing another Mill to take another one of his pieces.]

BJORN

"And you and your esteemed guard weren't kidding when you said you were going to make me work for a win. I've been able do to nothing but try and defend this entire game."

[Bjorn completes a Mill and Nasrin-Nush grins as he takes one of her pieces.]

NASRIN-NUSH

"That you have been struggling. That was the best move you could have made, but your doom is still sealed."

[They finish the game out with Nasrin-Nush winning.]

BJORN

"Do we have time for more? That was quite fun, much more interesting than pretending to read a book while nervously waiting for what comes next."

NASRIN-NUSH

"We do, but I'm much more interested in you telling me other ways this game or others have been useful to you in your travels."

BJORN

"Well, games are more fun if you can make stakes. Have something of value to win or lose. Gambling and being able to earn something is always handy."

NASRIN-NUSH

"Ugh. Bets and prize pots take away from the true enjoyment of playing for enjoyment's sake."

BJORN

"True, but for a person on hard times being clever and skillful might make the difference between going hungry or having a meal to survive until tomorrow."

NASRIN-NUSH

"People shouldn't have to stoop to such levels just to survive. Society should be able to support and protect against such things happening."

BJORN

"You're right. It's true that people shouldn't have to resort to such methods for survival, but should never goes very far in reality. Especially with how greedy many people can be. Now for as long as I've been in your kingdom the only thing that shouldn't be happening is the needless deaths of bold and rash young men."

NASRIN-NUSH

"Ugh not this again! I cannot undo the past and you yourself said you understood why I went through such drastic measures. You yourself may yet wind up just like one of those who have come before you!"

BJORN

"True, and now more than before I hope that I don't meet that fate. First I began this quest in the name of justice for those who have been lost. Now I am glad to have just gotten the chance to meet and know you, your highness."

NASRIN-NUSH

[Her mouth opens in surprise and she slightly blushes before shaking her head and replacing this with frustration and disdain.]

"Enough! This time I am playing to lose. You cannot hope to out strategize me to make sure that I win where you lose as I am playing to make sure that you win and I lose. It does not matter if you go first or second."

BJORN

"Fair enough, but I raise my standards of my own strategy. I will play to a draw. I may not win, but I will ensure that you will not lose."

[Bjorn places his first piece.]

NASRIN-NUSH

"Play to a... draw? You cannot just force it so the game always ends in a draw!" *[They each begin placing stones.]*

BJORN

"Ah, but you can! This is a trick that has come in useful to me before. In royal courts to the most common of taverns."

WATCHMAN

"See your highness? Your father wasn't wrong in insisting that you learn more courtly games. This one is for commoners, surely you'd like more games meant for the nobility."

NASRIN-NUSH

"Quiet! I've had full enough of those games. This one is much more engaging to me."

[They are now in the second stage sliding stones, but making no Mills.]

BJORN

"Draw."

NASRIN-NUSH

"You got lucky! Such trickery! It's because you went first, not again! Another game! Now! You better not have gone easy on me in the first round and *let* me win!"

[She sets down her first stone for the third game, anger rising to her voice and face.]

BJORN

"Oh I never allow anyone to win just by chance, believe that about me. Not even children. If you let someone win they will not learn how to lose and being a poor loser is one of the worst things a person could be."

[Continues to play with her while talking.]

NASRIN-NUSH

"Quiet, knave, I will not allow you your draw!"

BJORN

"Ah, if you figure that out can you still refuse me a draw, but guarantee yourself to lose and force me to win?"

WATCHMAN

"Maybe this was a mistake. Maybe we should just go back and wait with your family before the banquet..."
NASRIN-NUSH
"You be quiet, too! I need to concentrate!"
BJORN
"Draw."

NASRIN-NUSH
"IMPOSSIBLE! AGAIN! ANOTHER ROUND! I DON'T CARE WHO GOES FIRST!"
[There is a knock on the door.]
PUCCINIO
"Esteemed sir? Is everything alright in there? I came to tell you the banquet will be commencing shortly, we just must find the, ah, uh, locate the, uh, princess to be ready in her throne when you enter."

BJORN
[Bjorn opens the door and looks out and smiles.]
"I'm great, everything is great. I will be ready when you come to collect me."
PUCCINIO
"Good, good then I must go make the final arrangements."
WATCHMAN
"Come now Your Grace, we must go."
NASRIN-NUSH
"Not until I find out how he has deceived me!"
BJORN
"That explanation takes many, many hours and I'm not quite sure I would ever want to reveal my secret."
NASRIN-NUSH

"WHAT?! I have been playing and studying this game for years! I order you to explain how you pulled that off. It's a fluke. We will play again and I will figure out how you did it!"

BJORN

"You order me to, your highness? Or you'll what? Order my head to be chopped off? No. This is my gift and puzzle to you. If I win you will be happy to marry me because then we will have many opportunities for you to learn my way. If I am to lose your challenges then you will be happy in that you will not have to be married, but my secret strategy will go to the grave with me."

NASRIN-NUSH

"I think you are the most insufferable oaf I have ever had the unfortunate displeasure of meeting! I have never been so insulted! So enraged! I! I! Guard! Come now with me!"

[Nasrin-Nush storms out of the room with the Watchman following behind shooting an apologetic face towards Bjorn. As they disappear off stage Puccinio appears again and leads Bjorn back to the throne room.]

Scene 2

[Bjorn enters a dining hall full of long tables with wonderful food. At the far end the king and Nasrin-Nush are seated. He is led by the servants up to a table facing them. Everyone is standing behind their chairs, waiting for the king to have everyone sit down together.]

KING MIKHAIL

"Welcome, welcome! This banquet feast is in honor of you dear sir who has taken up the quest to earn my daughter's hand in marriage. It has been a long time coming and I think I speak for all of my subjects when I saw that this is a wonderful and blessed day!"

NASRIN-NUSH

"Now, now, father, don't treat him as son-in-law just yet. He still has to make it through dinner. I'm not done testing my young suitor. You told me that I have final say over who I marry so I can find a true and worthy match."

KING MIKHAIL

"Of course, my dear, of course, but after so many years can't you see that maybe all of your hard work is paying off and you've finally found a worthy partner? This, uh, what is your name and where do you hail from?"

BJORN

"My most esteemed and benevolent king, I am at you and your daughter's utmost service. However, I must apologize that I cannot reveal my identity just as of yet. For while I am confident in myself and my skills, there is more than just my life at stake right now. The more I say, the more I endanger others and I apologize again that is not a satisfactory answer for you right now. If I am successful in this test then I will be safe to reveal my identity and so much more."

KING MIKHAIL

"So be it! Our mystery suitor has made it this far. Let us continue our evening and we will see what happens before the sunrises. Everyone may be seated and enjoy!"

[Everyone sits down and begins to eat. The servants are circling around. The executioner is standing at the door out of the feasting hall, the watchman is standing guard behind the princess's chair. There are others there eating and enjoying the feast and musicians playing for others to dance.]

NASRIN-NUSH

[She speaks to the guard behind her and no one else hears their conversation.] "Trusted Guard. Take my pearl earrings here to our bold guest. Let's see if he can solve what to do with them next."

WATCHMAN

"Immediately your grace!"

[The guard crosses the stage to Bjorn.]

"Sir. These are from the princess we both adore."

[Guard returns to stand behind Nasrin-Nush.]

BJORN

"Ah hah! She has started the next riddle."

[Bjorn glances up at the spot where Nasrin-Nush is drinking from her cup and smirking towards him, knowing how tricky her puzzle must be.]

"Let's see, let me weigh these in my hands. Hmm. Yes, I think I know what to do."

[Bjorn reaches down and pulls out a pouch. He carefully pours out a tiny pile of pearls and spends a moment looking over each of them. He adds three to the two sent by Nasrin-Nush. When finished he gets the attention of one of the servants.]

"My good sir, would you please deliver these to the fiery lady sitting next to her father?"

PUCCINIO

"Right away, sir!"

[Puccinio hands the five pearls to the princess across the room.]

KING MIKHAIL

"What's this then, daughter? You're barely eating or drinking. You've kept the most impolite death stare on the young suitor. Are you really so anxious to end his life? Or mayhaps you're finally eager to be wed?"

NASRIN-NUSH

"Oh father, I have waited a long time for this and even your nagging can't ruin this for me. Let me enjoy this evening as he surely must be."

[From under the table Nasrin-Nush pulls out a scale to weigh the pearls against a stone she had used to find the pair of earrings.]

KING MIKHAIL

"Daughter, are you bringing science equipment to dinner again?! I thought we had discussed that there is a time and place for experimenting and royal dinner parties are neither!"

NASRIN-NUSH

"You have your idea of proper dinner activities and I have mine. He's passed the first part of this test so just be joyful and eat and drink for both of us. I sent him two pearls and he found their matches and has multiplied the riches I have given to him."

KING MIKHAIL

"Oh well then if that's where we stand in this contest I'll let it slide. Afterwards, please dear, keep your dinner time separate from your studies."

[Nasrin-Nush pulls a mortar and pestle out from under the table where the scale had been. She starts to put all five pearls into it.]

"Daughter! What is it now that you're doing? How much other equipment are you hiding?!"

NASRIN-NUSH

"Oh patience Father, patience. This all will pay off in good time. Either for you or for me. If I can't have a husband that will be an equal to me I will find one who is so beneath my station that I can control and ignore and it will be just like I'm alone still."

[She begins to grind up all five pearls into a fine dust and mixes in two spoonfuls of sugar from the table and smiles sweetly and dangerously down at Bjorn.]

"Guard. Please go now and take this bowl to our guest and see how he figures out this next test."

WATCHMAN

"Right away your highness."

[The Watchman crosses the stage again and hands the bowl of sugary pearl dust to Bjorn.]

"So far so good, my friend. I have no idea what she wants or expects from you this time."

BJORN

"Not to worry, friend. I will solve this as I have solved the others. Go back now to your mistress and wait."

[Bjorn studies the powder mixture until Antonio walks by.]

"My good sir, I know you are quite busy, but if I could trouble you for a glass of milk I would be most appreciative."

ANTONIO

"At once sir! I will return momentarily!"

[Antonio walks off stage and back on with a glass of milk.]

"Here you are sir, what else may I help you with?"

BJORN

"Give me a moment, just a moment."

[Bjorn carefully stirs the pearl powder mixture into the milk until the sugar dissolves, but the pearl dust settles in the bottom of the cup so the audience sees.] "There! That should take care of that, please send this glass to the most wondrous lady with my humblest admirations."

[Bjorn shoots a grin, wink, and nod towards Nasrin-Nush and she scoffs and rolls her eyes.]

ANTONIO

"A gift from the young man to you my grace."

NASRIN-NUSH

"Thank you, you are dismissed."

[Nasrin-Nush drinks the milk daintily with her eyes shut.]

"Clever man. Very clever and wily indeed, let's see if it matches." [

Nasrin-Nush scoops the remaining powder out of the bottom of the cup and weighs it on the scale with stones equaling the weight of the five original pearls.]

KING MIKHAIL

"Again with the scales! Who are you? Some sort of common merchant's daughter? Why must you be interested and curious in all except for that which would serve both of us well?"

NASRIN-NUSH

"What I endeavor in is to not only serve you well, but also all people in our kingdom and our fellow kingdoms, Father. Be patient and leave me to my testing. You will be pleased to know that our young suitor has now passed the second test."

KING MIKHAIL

"Wonderful news, dear, because I for one have no idea what you are doing to test this poor lad."

NASRIN-NUSH

"More the pity for you, Father, although it is by your wisdom you've allowed me to educate myself so. I will always appreciate and be glad of that greatest gift you have given to me. Guard once more I give you a gift to take over to our guest."

[She removes her ruby ring from her hand and gives it to the Watchman.]

KING MIKHAIL

"My little flower! You do not mean to use your mother's ring as a tool to trap this man in his death? That is her most favorite jewel!"

NASRIN-NUSH

"I am quite aware of its importance, Father, if he passes my tests then he shall be family and his hands an extension of mine and my hands an extension of his. If he fails, I'll just get it off his corpse when the executioner is finished with him." *[Nasrin-Nush nods and winks at the Executioner who tips his axe and bows from across the room.]*

KING MIKAHIL

"Sometimes I do wonder if your heart is completely frozen with ice my fiery daughter. I love you with all my being, but your coldness worries me."

[Nasrin-Nush comforts her father by patting his hand.]

WATCHMAN

"It's still going well my friend. Here is the latest gift to you from our sweet princess."

[The Watchman hands Bjorn the ring and returns to stand behind the princess.]

BJORN

"Ah! A fine and rare ruby!

[Bjorn places the ring on his finger]

"Let's find something just as well to match this one of a kind gem."

[Bjorn pulls out two more bags and removes a ring from one with an empty setting and a luminous and glowing pearl from the other. He squeezes the glowing pearl into the ring setting. He sees Giacomo passing by.]

"Good sir, could I bother you to please take this precious ring to the most wondrous lady?"

GIACOMO

"Of course my good friend, of course! Right away!"

[Giacomo takes the ring and brings it up to the princess and bows and returns to his duties.]

KING MIKHAIL

"What a wonderfully beautiful and luminous stone! Daughter, such a glowing light coming from a pearl? This is some kind of amazing magic of which I've never seen!"

NASRIN-NUSH

"It is quite rare, father, I will give you that."

[She places the glowing ring on her finger.]

"However, I have seen it's kind before."

[She removes a pearl necklace from under her dress and breaks the string. She piles the pearls carefully on a plate on the table and pulls out a pearl glowing just as fiercely as the one in the ring. She pulls the pearl out of the ring and begins to string them onto a smaller chain that was also under the table.]

KING MIKHAIL

"First weights, then grinding, and now jewel crafting. I don't know why I have ever expected to have one normal royal meal with you. I thought now that you are an adult and have had time to focus on your silly things that you could compartmentalize."

NASRIN-NUSH

"I am my own true self and being true to myself is all I can ever do, Father. I love you and this is almost complete. It would be a great tragedy for our young man to fail on the last puzzle I now present to him. Don't ruin this for him, now, with your complaining. Guard one more time please take these to our guest. Thank you."

[Nasrin-Nush hands the pearls on the chain to the Watchman and watches as they hand them over to the prince.]

BJORN

"Thank you friend."

[Bjorn takes the pearls from the Watchman and they return to stand behind the princess.]

"So she had a match for my wondrous pearl. These pearls that were gifted unto the sea just as the Pleiades were gifted into the night sky. These two are perhaps the only two such pearls in the entire world and must truly be a sign that we are, in fact, destined to be together."

[Bjorn pulls out a plain, blue, glass bead from his pouch. He strings it with the pearls so it sits in between them, twinkling in their soft glow. This time he stands and carefully approaches the seat of Nasrin-Nush and taking a knee hands her the string with pearls and bead.]

NASRIN-NUSH

"While no great gem or pearl could match these two, you send me a simple and plain bead of blue glass I could get at any common market stand." *[As she talks she sets the pearls into her earrings and ties the blue bead on her wrist as a bracelet.]* "Rich or poor,wise or fool, all of us do need to protect and harden ourselves against the evil eye. In this the best protection is a blue bauble plain and simple. Father, go ahead and arrange the wedding, I have played with fortune long enough. I have finally and graciously been blessed with a man worthy of sharing my life with. "

Scene 3

[The next day the palace and city are full of celebration and revelry. King Harold and Kari stand at an altar with the Watchman. Giacomo, Antonio, and Puccino are preparing the ceremony and the music begins with the Executioner walking down the aisle throwing flowers.]

KARI

While I am sad that I will not be able to marry our dear Prince Bjorn, I am overjoyed that he has survived and found happiness and joy.

KING HAROLD

Indeed it was my greatest fear that I would again lose my son after we were separated after the disaster that befell our homeland. When life seems its bleakest the fates will reward the steadfast with joy and fulfillment at the end.

WATCHMAN

I'm just thrilled that I don't have to make that perilous hike between two fortresses each week and can actually have time for myself again. While I adore our most joyous Princess, I truly miss, ahem, meeting new people.

[The Watchman winks shyly at Kari and they wave back with a small smile]

[At this point the princess has made it to the end of the aisle and is helped up by her father and handed off to Bjorn]

KING MIKHAIL

My loyal subjects! Today is a great day that has been a long time coming with much anticipation. My most precious flower of a daughter has finally found a garden of a suitor worthy for her to live with. She is as lovely and beautiful as her mother was, and exceeds all of our scholars and magi in wisdom and knowledge. I present to you the worthy Norseman Prince Bjorn, his most noble father King Harold, and their faithful companion Kari. They have traveled for many years to come to our kingdom and fate has led them to join our family through the love of Nasrin-Nush and Bjorn.

Truly we are a blessed nation and people to have such generous, kind, and thoughtful future rulers to be joined in marriage today.

[Bjorn and Nasrin-Nush kneel before King Mikhail and the wedding wreath crowns are brought out. Bjorn's wreath is made of rowan, holly, and juniper leaves and the Watchman stands behind him with it facing towards Kari who holds Nasrin-Nush's wreath crown was made of red heather, guelder rose berries, and fiery sunflowers.)

Today you are crowned to one another in marriage and in front of your future subjects. They may see you as you see one another in your hearts and souls as destiny has brought all of us here to this most joyful moment. Rise and let us commence the celebration!

[The crowd cheers and throws flower petals as the newly wed couple proceeds out, followed by the two old kings waving at the people, The Watchman and Kari link arms, followed by the Executioner, Giacomo, Antonio, and Puccinio.]

<u>Epilogue</u>

We hope you enjoyed this modern take on an ancient tale. Nasrin-Nush and Bjorn ruled for many and a happy year with their joyful kingdom prosperous and mighty. They also enjoyed learning and teaching each other. And yes, eventually Bjorn told Nasrin-Nush the secrets of the way to end every game of Mills in a draw.

Don't miss out!

Visit the website below and you can sign up to receive emails whenever Casey Nash publishes a new book. There's no charge and no obligation.

https://books2read.com/r/B-A-IXLT-RWCYB

About the Author

Casey lives in Tucson, Arizona where he grew up. He is a parent to three wonderful children and worked many positions in teaching and education. His hobbies are gardening, gaming, reading, and coming up with imaginative stories.

www.ingramcontent.com/pod-product-compliance
Lightning Source LLC
Chambersburg PA
CBHW021349150726
47989CB00005B/2175